Luella Agnes Owen

Cave Regions of the Ozarks and Black Hills

Luella Agnes Owen

Cave Regions of the Ozarks and Black Hills

ISBN/EAN: 9783337327354

Printed in Europe, USA, Canada, Australia, Japan

Cover: Foto ©Andreas Hilbeck / pixelio.de

More available books at **www.hansebooks.com**

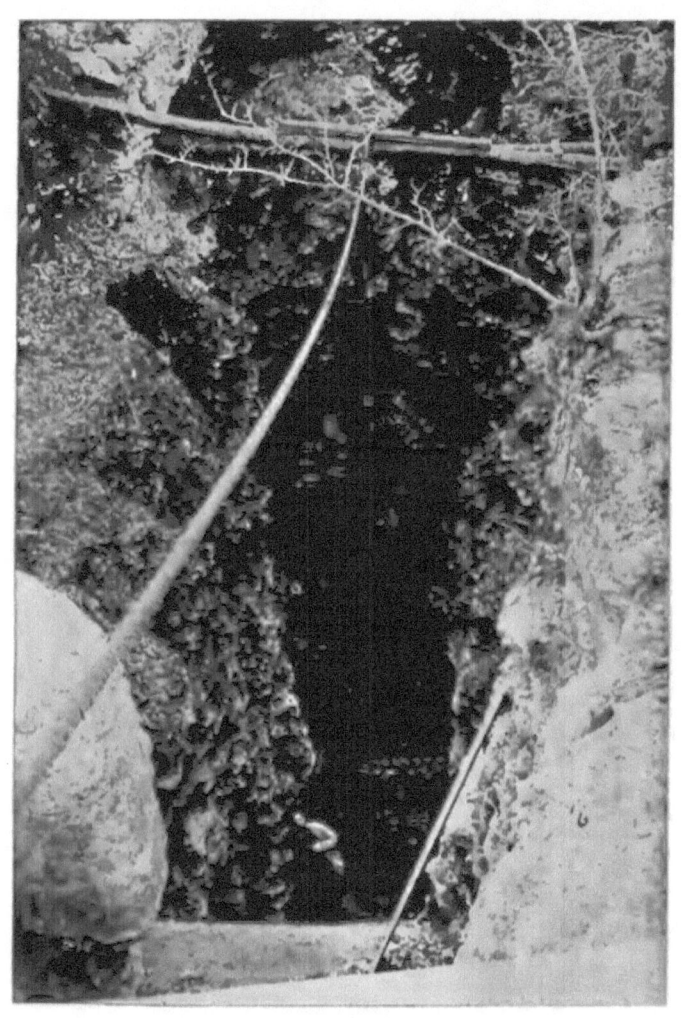

ENTRANCE TO MARBLE CAVE.
Page 25.

Cave Regions

of the

Ozarks and Black Hills

BY

LUELLA AGNES OWEN.

*Membre titulaire de la Société de Spéléologie, and
Fellow of the American Geographical Society.*

CINCINNATI,
THE EDITOR PUBLISHING CO.
1898.

TO
MY MOTHER
THIS BOOK IS AFFECTIONATELY
DEDICATED.

CONTENTS.

THE OZARKS AND BLACK HILLS.

———

CHAPTER I.

A GENERAL VIEW.

" O'er mountains bright with snow and light,
We crystal hunters speed along,
While grots, and caves, and icy waves,
Each instant echo to our song;
And when we meet with stores of gems
We grudge not kings their diadems."
—*Thomas Moore.*

The southern half of the State of Missouri,
and the Black Hills of South Dakota, offer
exceptionally delightful regions for the study of
caves, or Speleology as it has been named, and
the sister sciences of geology and geography at
the same time. In fact it is impossible to study
either without giving attention to the other
two, and therefore, instead of being separate
sciences, they are the three branches of a great
scientific trinity.

The regions here referred to enjoy the advantage, and at the same time suffer the disadvantage, of being comparatively little known to the ever restless tide of tourists who naturally hail with pleasure the announcement that some easily accessible, and thoroughly charming spot, has escaped their attention altogether, with a marvelous store of attractions which are both extremely old and wholly new.

Each of these regions has a peculiar geological history not repeated in any other portions of the earth's surface : each is blessed with its own peculiar style of beautiful scenery : and each vies with the other and all the world besides for the supremacy of its truly wonderful caves. Yet it should be well understood that the claims are not based on an unworthy spirit of rivalry, nor any desire to deny the greatness and beauty of already famous members of the Cave family. It is simply an announcement that the family is much larger than has been generally supposed, and the more recently presented members worthy of the full measure of distinguished honors.

The geological authorities of both states have for many years mentioned the beauty and importance of these regions, and urged their claims to public attention, but have been prevented, by the pressure of other duties, from giving to the caves such careful study and full reports as they deserve, as it would have been a pleasure to give, and as has been possible in states of less extent where the general work of the department is more advanced, and the volume of tourist travel created an early demand for scientific explanation.

Without any great difficulty we can understand the process of cave excavation by the action of percolating acidulated water on the limestone, and its subsequent removal as the volume of surface drainage diverted to the new channel gradually increased. But it is not so easy to offer a reason for the varied forms with which the caves are afterwards decorated. Why is it the charmed waters do not leave the evidence of their slow passage only in plain surfaces of varying widths, and the stalactites and stalagmites whose formation we can readily account for? And why do not the deposits take the same forms in all caves with only such variations as would naturally result from differences in topography? The law is written, but in unfamiliar characters that render our reading slow and uncertain. Yet it is conspicuously noticeable that those caves showing the most delicately fragile and wonderfully varied forms of decoration are those traversed by the most sweeping and changeable, or even reversible, currents of air; which might lead to the conclusion that the moisture is sprayed or converted into a light, misty vapor, and then deposited in exactly the same manner as the beautiful frost-work at Niagara: the direction and force of the current determining the location of the frail deposits.

Since the largest and most important caves occur in limestone, a little special attention to the cause of their occurrence there may serve to show that although speleology has only recently received its name and been elevated to the rank of a separate and independent science, it is one of the earth's ancient institutions.

Our geologists, who have unearthed many secrets not dreamed of even in Humboldt's "good phylosopy," have settled the question of how the different kinds of caves were formed, according to the character of rocks they are in, or their location and depth, and the natural agencies to whose action they show signs of having been subjected.

Dr. H. C. Hovey, in his "Celebrated American Caverns," says: "In visiting caves of large extent, one is at first inclined to regard the long halls, huge rifts, deep pits and lofty domes, as evidences of great convulsions of nature, whereby the earth has been violently rent asunder. But, while mechanical forces have had their share in the work, as has been shown, the main agent in every case has been the comparatively gentle, invisible gas known as carbonic acid. This is generated by the decay of animal and vegetable substances, and is to a

considerable degree soluble in water. Under
ordinary circumstances one measure of water
will absorb one measure of carbonic acid; and
the eye will detect no difference in its appearance. Under pressure the power of absorption
is rapidly increased, until the water thus sur-
charged has an acid taste, and effervesces on
flowing from the earth, as in Saratoga water.

"Rain-water, falling amid leaves and grass,
and sinking into the soil, absorbs large quantities of carbonic acid. On reaching the under-
lying limestone, the latter is instantly attacked
by the acidulated water in which it is dissolved
and carried away.

"It is agreed among geologists, amazing as
the statement may seem, that the immense
caverns of Virginia, Kentucky and Indiana,
including Mammoth Cave itself (the largest of
all), were eaten out of the solid mass of limestone by the slow, patient, but irresistible action
of acidulated water."

Professor N. S. Shaler says: "The existence
of deep caverns is a sign that the region has
long been above the sea."

Through the kindness of Professor C. J. Norwood, Chief Inspector and Curator of the
Geological Department of Kentucky, it is possible to quote the first official report made on the
caves of that state and published in 1856, in
Volume I., Kentucky Geological Survey Reports.

Dr. Norwood says: "Referring to the 'Sub-carboniferous Limestone' (now known as the St. Louis group of the Mississippian series), Dr. Owen says: 'The southern belt of this formation is wonderfully cavernous, especially in its upper beds, which being more argillaceous, and impregnated with earths and alkalies, are disposed to produce salts, which oozing through the pores of the stone effloresce on its surface, and thus tend to disintegrate and scale off, independent of the solvent effects of the carbonated water. Beneath overhanging ledges of limestone, quantities of fine earthy rubbish can be seen, weathered off from such causes. In these I have detected sulphate of lime, sulphate of magnesia, nitrate of lime, and occasionally sulphate of soda. The tendency which some calcareous rocks have to produce nitrate of lime is, probably, one of the greatest causes of disintegration.'"

"Most extensive subterranean areas thus have been excavated or undermined in Edmonson, Hart, Grayson, Butler, Logan, Todd, Christian and Trig. In the vicinity of Green River, in the first of these counties, the known avenues of the Mammoth Cave amount to two hundred and twenty-three, the united length of the whole being estimated, by those best acquainted with the Cave, at one hundred and fifty miles; say that the average width and height of these passages amount to seven yards each way, which is perhaps near the truth; this would give upwards of twelve million cubic yards of cavernous space which has been excavated through the agency of calcareous waters and atmospheric vicissitudes."

Page 169: "On the south side of Green River the platform of limestone forming the descent into Mammoth Cave is two hundred and thirty-two feet above Green River."

"The entrance to the cave, being thirty-eight feet lower than this bed of limestone, is one hundred and ninty-four .feet above Green River. In the above two hundred and thirty-two feet there are several heavy masses of sandstone, viz: at one hundred and twenty-five, one hundred and forty-five, one hundred and fifty, one hundred and sixty and two hundred and fifteen feet, but it is probable that most of these have tumbled from higher positions in the hill, as no alterations of sandstone have been observed at these levels in the cave. From an elevation of from two hundred and forty to two hundred and fifty feet, the prevalent rock is sandstone without pebbles, which can be seen extending up to three hundred and twelve feet to the foundation of the Cave Hotel. The united thickness of the limestone beds on this part of Green River, is about two hun-

dred and thirty feet, capped with eighty
feet of sandstone. About midway of the
section on this part of Green River, are
limestones of an obscure oolitic structure, but
no true oolite was observed. Many of these
limestones are of such composition as to be
acted on freely by the elements of the atmosphere, which, in the form of nitric acid, combine with the earthy and alkaline bases of calcareous rock, and give rise to the formation of
nitrates with the liberation of carbonic acid;
hence the disintegrated rubbish of the caves
yields nitrate of potash after being treated with
the ley of ashes and subsequent evaporation of
the saline lixivium. The wonderfully cavernous character of the subcarboniferous limestones of the Green River valley, and, indeed,
of these particular members of the subcarboniferous group throughout a great part of its range
in Kentucky and Indiana, is due in a great
measure to this cause, together with the solvent
and eroding effects of water charged with carbonic acid. The 'rock-houses' frequently encountered both in this formation and in the
limestones of Silurian date, are produced by
similar causes; the more easily disintegrated
beds gradually crumbling away, while the more
durable remain in overhanging ledges. By the
oxidation of other elements, sulphates of oxide
of iron and alkalies result, which, by double

decomposition, with carbonate of lime, give rise to the formation of gypsums which appears in the form of rosettes, festoons and various other imitative forms on the walls and ceilings of the caves. Crystallizations of sulphate of soda and sulphate of magnesia are not uncommon, both in some of the caves and in sheltered situations under shelving rocks.''

The explanations thus given of the excavation and subsequent refilling and decoration of the limestone caves of Kentucky and Indiana apply equally well to those of other states; but it is to be remembered that at the time of Dr. Owen's report, onyx, the most beautiful and valuable of dripstones, had not yet been discovered in the United States; while now especially fine deposits are known in California, Utah, Missouri, South Dakota and Arkansas; the Missouri supply being exceptionally valuable on account of the marvelous delicacy and beauty of its coloring; nor can it soon be exhausted, as deposits have been found in eight counties and further exploration will no doubt discover more.

Concerning the Subcarboniferous, or Mississippian Series in Part I., Vol. IV., Missouri Geological Survey, Dr. C. R. Keyes says: '' In the great interior basin of the Mississippi the basal series is exposed more or less continuously over

broad areas, extending from northern Iowa to
Alabama, and from Ohio to Mexico."

While this broadly extended series of limestone is honey-combed in many places and all
directions by wonderful caverns, those of the
Ozark regions in Missouri, although comparatively little known, are well worth knowing,
and are possibly the most ancient limestone
caves in the world. Of the region in which
they occur, Dr. Keyes, in the volume last quoted,
says: "The chief typographical feature of the
state has long been known in the Ozark uplift, a
broad plateau with gentle quaquaversal slopes
rising to a height of more than one thousand
five hundred feet above mean tide, and
extending almost entirely across the southern part of the district. On all sides
the borders of this highland area are deeply
grooved by numberless streams flowing in narrow gorges. Against its nucleus of very ancient granites and porphyries the Ozark
series of magnesian limestone was laid
down. Then the area occupied by these
rocks was elevated, and around its margins
were deposited successively the other members
of the Paleozoic. The Ozark region was
thus the first land to appear within the
borders of the present state of Missouri." He
further says: "Although it has long been known
that the Magnesian Limestones are older than the

Trenton, and that they lie immediately upon
and against the Archæan crystallines uncomform-
ably, their exact geological age has always
remained unsettled. There seems to be but
little doubt, however, that part of the series is
equivalent to the Calciferous of other regions.
It is also pretty well determined that certain of
the lower beds, all below the 'Saccharoidal'
Sandstone perhaps, are representatives of the
Upper Cambrian or Potsdam. These conclusions
appear well grounded both upon stratigraphical
and faunal evidence. The rocks of the Ozark
region have not as yet received the necessary
detailed study to enable the several lines of de-
markation to be drawn with certainty. This
investigation is now being carried on as rapidly
as possible, and promises very satisfactory and
interesting results in the near future.''

"The early geological reports represent the
Magnesian Limestone series as made up of seven
members. . Following Swallow, these may be
briefly described in the present connection. Be-
ginning at the top, they are:
First Magnesian Limestone.
First, or Saccharoidal Sandstone.
Second Magnesian Limestone.
Second Sandstone.
Third Magnesian Limestone.
Third Sandstone.
Fourth Limestone,''

"The Fourth" Magnesian Limestone, or lowest
number of the Ozark series recognized, has its
typical exposures along the Niangua and Osage
rivers in Morgan and Camden counties.

Professor Swallow, in his Missouri Geological
Survey Reports I. and II, 1853 and 1854, says:
"Caves, natural bridges and subterranean
streams occur in the valley of the Osage and its
tributaries." The same authority of forty years
ago also mentions that "Some of the grandest
scenery in the State is produced by the high
castellated and mural bluffs of this (Third Magnesian Limestone) Formation, on the Niangua
and the Osage." Another reference to the
scenery on these rivers describes it as "Wild
and grand, beautiful and unique ;" with "gaudy-
colored bluffs." In the section on building
materials he remarks; "One of the most
desirable of the Missouri marbles is in the Third
Magnesian Limestone on the Niangua. It is
fine-grained, crystalline, silico-magnesian limestone of a light drab, slightly tinged with peach-
blossom, and beautifully clouded with the same
hue or flesh color. It is twenty feet thick and
crops out in the bluffs. This marble is rarely
surpassed in the qualities which fit it for ornamental architecture."

The Ozarks in the extreme southern portion of
the state are even less known to the world, but
the scenery is grand, the climate delightful,

and the caves worthy of a visit for themselves alone. The State of Missouri being one third larger than England, and of equal size to Switz-erland, Holland, Belgium and Denmark combined, it is not surprising that interesting discoveries are still to be expected.

The climate is so varied on account of the range in latitude and altitude, and the natural resources are so great, the claim has been made that if the State were surrounded by an impas-sable wall, its citizens need not be deprived of any article necessary to a refined and luxurious mode of living: and according to Mr. Henry Gannett in "The Building of a Nation," the population in 1890 was 73.42 per cent. native whites of native parents, the colored a little less than 6 per cent., and nearly two-thirds of the balance, native born of parents, one or both of whom were foreign.

Although the Ozark region has not yet received sufficient attention to dull its charm for the explorer, the fact has been established that its earliest sedimentary rocks are of the Cambrian Age and still occupy mainly the position in which they were originally deposited. Therefore we need not be surprised to discover that some, at least, of the excavations are proportionately ancient; and that the Natural Bridges are the last remaining positive evidence of their former existence and final collapse. That the Natural

Bridges of Missouri mark the destruction of
more ancient caves than the one preserved to
geological history by Virginia's grand attraction,
seems quite evident. The greater age of the
rocks indicates the possibility of earlier excavation while their undisturbed position suggests
that destruction resulted, not from violent earth
movement, but from the slow action of agencies
requiring long periods of time.

Before proceeding to a discussion of the
caves visited personally for the gratification of
private interest, it is desirable to know what
attention has been given to the subject, inci-
dentally, in the course of regular official duty on
the Missouri Geological Survey.

CAVES DESCRIBED IN THE STATE REPORTS.

Although many unknown caves must yet be
discovered in the imperfectly explored portions
of the vast Ozark forests, these finds are already
so numerous as to seldom attract attention
according to their just deserts.

One of the comparatively recent of these discoveries is Crystal Cave, at Joplin, described on
page 566, Vol. VII., Missouri Geological Survey
Report 1894.* It was opened in the lower work-
ings of a shaft of the Empire Zinc Company, and
"The entire surface of the cave, top, sides
and bottom, is lined with calcite crystals, so

---

*Lead and Zinc. Prof. C. R. Keyes.

closely packed together as to form a continuous
sheet and most of them of great size, and well
formed faces. Scalenohedra as much as two feet
long are sometimes seen, and others a foot or
more in length are common. Planes or crystal
ghosts, sometimes with pyrite crystals, marking
stages of growth in the calcite crystals, are often
distinguishable. The entire absence of anything like stalactites is noticeable, and together
with the presence of the crystals, show that the
cave was completely filled with water during
their growth." In the same volume, all those
counties in the extreme southwest corner of the
state, whose geological age has not heretofore
been considered positively determined, are
mapped as Lower Carboniferous, and Lower Silurian, with the Coal Measures covering portions of
Barton and Jasper and appearing in a few small,
scattered spots in Dade, Polk, Green and Christian counties, and some scanty lines of Devonian
fringing the edges of the Silurian in Barton and
McDonald.

Other State reports make mention of many
caves and fine springs, and also several natural
bridges worthy of special notice. In Mr. G. C.
Broadhead's report for 1873-1874, he gives a
short but interesting chapter on caves and water
supplies, in which he says that "Caves occur in
the Third Magnesian Limestone, Saccharoidal

Sandstone, Trenton, Lithographic, Encrinital and St. Louis Limestone.''

"In Eastern and Northeast Missouri there have not been found many large caves in the Encrinital Limestone, but the lower beds of this formation in Southwest Missouri often enclose very large caverns; among the latter may be included the caves of Green County with some in Christian and McDonald. Those in McDonald I have not seen, but they are reported to be very extensive and probably are situated in the Encrinital Limestone.''

Under the head of "Special Descriptions" he says: "On Sac River, in the north part of Green County, we find a cave with two entrances, one at the foot of a hill, opening toward Sac River, forty-five feet high and eighty feet wide. The other entrance is from the hill-top, one hundred and fifty feet back from the face of the bluff. These two passages unite. The exact dimensions of the cave are not known, but there are several beautiful and large rooms lined with stalactites and stalagmites which often assume both beautiful and grotesque life-like forms. The cave has been explored for several hundred yards, showing the formations to be thick silicious beds of the Lower Carboniferous formations.''

"Knox cave, in Green County, is said to be of

large dimensions. I have not seen it, but some of its stalactites are quite handsome.''

"Wilson's Creek sinks beneath the Limestone and appears again below.''

"There are several caves near Ozark, Christian County, which issue from the same formation as those in Green County. On a branch of Finly Creek a stream disappears in a sink, appearing again three-quarters of a mile southeast through an opening sixty feet high by ninety-eight feet wide. Up stream the cave continues this size for a hundred yards and then decreases in size, and for the next quarter of a mile further it is generally ten by fourteen feet wide. A very clear, cool stream passes out, in which by careful search crawfish without eyes can be found.''

"There is another cave a few miles south of Ozark, and another ten miles southeast occurs in the Magnesian Limestone.''

"In Boone County there are several caves in the Encrinital Limestone. Conner's, the largest, is said to have been explored for a distance of eight miles.''

"In Pike and Lincoln there are several small caves occurring in the upper beds of Trenton Limestone, which are often very cavernous. On Sulphur Fork of Cuivre, there is a cave and Natural Bridge, to which parties for pleasure often resort. The bridge is tubular with twenty feet between the walls, and is one hundred feet long."

"At J. P. Fisher's on Spencer Creek, Ralls County, there is a cave having an entrance of ninety feet wide by twenty feet high. The Lower Trenton beds occupy the floor, with the upper cavernous beds above. On the bluff, at a distance of one hundred and fifty yards back, there is a sink-hole which communicates with the cave. Within the cave is a cool, clear spring of water, and Mr. F. said he could keep meat fresh there for six weeks during midsummer."

"The Third Magnesian Limestone which occupies such a large portion of Southwest Missouri, often contains very large caves. One of them, known as Friede's cave, is six or eight miles Northwest of Rolla, on Cave Spring Creek."

"It is said to have been explored for several miles, but I only passed in a few hundred yards. The stalactites here are very beautiful, assuming the structure of satin spar. A very clear stream of water issues out. West of the Gasconade, on Clifty Creek, is a remarkable Natural Bridge which I have elsewhere described in Geological Survey of Missouri, 1855–71, page 16."

"Mr. Meek speaks of a large and interesting cave on Tavern Creek, in Miller County. Dr. Shumard estimates a cave on Bryant's Fork, in Ozark County, to be a mile and a half long."

This description of Dr. Shumard's is in the Geological Survey of Missouri, 1855–71, page 196, where he says:

"The entrance is thirty-five feet wide and thirty feet high, and is situated at the foot of a perpendicular cliff, and far above the water-level of Bryant. Just within the entrance it expands to sixty or seventy feet, with a height of about fifty feet; and this part of the cave has been used by the citizens of the county as a place for holding camp-meeting. I estimated its length at not far short of one mile and a half. The main passage is in general quite spacious, the roof elevated, and the floor tolerably level, but often wet and miry. For some distance beyond the entrance there is not much to attract attention; but as we proceed, at the far extremity the chambers are quite as picturesque as the most noted of the well-known Mammoth Cave. The ceilings, sides and floor are adorned with a multitude of stalactites and stalagmites arranged in fanciful combinations, and assuming a variety of fantastic and beautiful forms."

Many of these caves contain niter, which occurs as a mineral and not as evidence of former animal occupation, it being found in the form of effervescenses on the walls. Dr. Shumard mentions several of this character in Pulaski County, the most noted being Niter Cave, in the Third Magnesian Limestone, with a wide

entrance thirty feet above the level of the Gasconade. On page 201, he also gives a charming
description of one of the immense springs that
are numerous in this region and that I have
never seen elsewhere. He says:

"Ozark County is bountifully supplied with
springs of the finest water, and some of them
of remarkably large size. The largest one is
situated near the North Fork, in T. 24, R. 11
W., Sec. 32, and is known under the name of the
Double Spring. It issues from near the base of
a bluff of Sandstone and Magnesian Limestone,
a few feet above the level of the North Fork.
This spring discharges an immense volume of
water, which is divided by a huge mass of Sandstone into two streams, with swift currents flowing
in opposite directions to join the North Fork
about one hundred and fifty yards distant from
the spring. I estimated the width of these
streams at not less than fifty yards. They are
separated from the North Fork by a pretty
wooded island one hundred yards long. The
upper stream affords a good mill-site. I am
informed that the quantity of water discharged
by this magnificent spring is not materially
diminished during the dryest seasons of the
year. The temperature of the water measured
at the edge of the spring, was found to be 56°;
the temperature of the air at the same time, 59°.
Other springs of considerable magnitude occur

in various portions of the county, giving rise to beautiful and limpid streams."

The descriptions of the Natural Bridge and Friede's cave, near Rolla, previously referred to as being on page 16 of the same volume, are as follows :

" On Clifty Creek found the chert bed of Sec. 21-5 occurring about sixty feet from the top of the Third Magnesian Limestone, with a road passing over its upper surface, presenting it very favorably for observation. It seemed here to be broken by vertical cracks into large rhomboidal blocks. Further up this creek in a wild and secluded spot, observed a Natural Bridge with six feet of this chert bed at its base, and Silicious Magnesian Limestone above. The span of this bridge is about thirty feet, an elevation of opening about fifteen feet above the water, the thickness of the rock above is about twelve feet, and width on top about fifteen feet. Two small streams come together, one from the west and another from the southwest. A point of the bluff on the south-west fork spans the northern fork, and terminates about sixty feet beyond in a sharp point; a few large masses of rock lie near the termination of the promontory, and fifty feet beyond, the bluffs of the opposite hills rise abruptly from the bottoms. The bluffs, both above and below, are very precipitous, the middle and lower beds

of the Third Magnesian Limestone forming perpendicular escarpments, frequently studded
with cedar, some occurring on top of the bridge.
A perfectly clear stream of water courses through
this valley. The bottoms near are overspread
with a dense growth of trees and vines, among
which latter I noticed the Muscadine grape.
The valley at this part being shut in by its perpendicular cliffs with not a path to guide the
traveler through the dense thickets, is wildly
picturesque and romantic in its loneliness."

Of the cave he says: "This cave is a quarter of a mile east of Cave Spring Creek, and has
a wide and elevated entrance; passing into it
a hundred yards or more, the passage narrows,
and in order to go further a stream of water
has frequently to be waded through; this passage has been followed by some persons several
miles without finding any object of interest;
but a few hundred yards from the entrance, by
diverging to the right, we enter a large chamber, studded with stalactites and stalagmites,
many uniting and forming solid columns of support. Many of these are very beautiful, and
often as white as alabaster. There are other
large rooms, but they possess no peculiar interest. Found large deposits of earth on the floor
having a saline taste."

Of the extensive pine forests in Ozark
County, he says: "The size and quality of the

timber will compare favorably with that of the celebrated pineries of Wisconsin and Minnesota."

In several other counties the pine is equally good, and other valuable timber everywhere abundant, although in a school geography published in 1838, the following descriptions of this region occur:

" The lowlands of the Mississippi are bounded by the region of the Ozark Mountains. With the exception of the alluvial tracts on the borders of the streams, it is extremely hilly and broken. The mountains rise from eight hundred to eighteen hundred feet above the streams, with rounded summits and often perpendicular cliffs, and have a rocky surface, which admits only a scanty growth of timber."   *   *

"Missouri is generally a region of prairies and table lands, much of which, as already described, is almost destitute of timber and water. It is crossed by the Ozark Mountains, which form a rugged tract of considerable extent. Earth-quakes are not infrequent in some parts of this state. The soil is not generally productive."

A comparison of these curious views with the latest official reports is highly amusing, as well as suggestive that, early impressions are liable to require modification.

In addition to the wonderful springs of pure water, there are numerous fine mineral springs, among which are a number of Epsom salt springs.

At Jacksonville, in Randolph County, there is a large mineral spring from which it is said an over-heated horse may drink all he will without injury. Epsom-salts, or Epsomite, frequently occurs, as does the Niter, in **a** crystalline form of the pure mineral, as an efflorescence on rocks in many of the caves and in other sheltered positions.

CHAPTER II.

Marble Cave, which is the finest yet explored in Missouri, is southeast of the center of Stone County, a short distance north of the picturesque White River. The nearest station is Marionville on the St. Louis and San Francisco railroad, and the drive of forty miles is delightful, but can be divided, into two of twenty each by a stop at Galena. The road, for the most part, is naturally macadamized and is through a most charming country whose roughness and beauty increase together as the journey advances. At first it winds along fertile valleys between wooded hills, crossing many times a shallow stream of water so clear as to afford no concealment for an occasional water-moccasin, whose bite is said to be not poisonous if inflicted under water, and which must be true because the horses showed not the least uneasiness.

The second week in May found the vegetation in its summer beauty; strawberries were ripe, and the weather without a fault.

Galena is pleasantly situated on the hills overlooking the James River, and is entirely in-

visible from the road by which it is approached
until a slight curve in the line of ascent ends
the first half of the journey with surprising
suddenness.   In the immediate vicinity there
are several small caves which are worthy of
attention and will be described later on.

To properly picture the twenty miles of
changing and charming views between Galena
and Marble Cave would require the light and
skillful touch of a special artist gifted with a
tangible perception of atmospheric values.
Gradually the road forsakes the pretty valleys
with their fields and streams, to take the summit of the hills and then be known as the "Ridge
Road," which affords a wide range of vision not
previously enjoyed, presenting scenes not to be
found reproduced elsewhere with any degree of
exactness.   Looking into the depth of the forest
as it slopes away on either side, the impression
is of a magnificent park, undefaced by what are
called improvements.   This effect is produced
by the scarcity, or entire absence of underbrush,
and a beautiful surface covering of grasses or
flowering plants of all kinds and colors, varied
here and there with masses of ferns of unusual
size and delicate beauty. The most unexpected and
lavish feature of the rich display is the many miles
of fragrant honeysuckle that grows only eighteen
inches high in the forest shade, but if trans-
planted to a sunny spot develops into the famil-

A Mill-Site Near Marble Cave.

iar vine. The most beautiful portion of all this
is called The Wilderness, and seems designed
for a National Park. Such a park reserve, even
if very small, could not fail to be a lasting
pleasure, since it would be more accessible to
large centers of population than other reserves,
and its most delightful seasons are spring and
autumn when the Yellowstone is under snow.

The distant view obtained through open spaces
is an undulating forest in all directions, being
apparently both trackless and endless. The
great variety of greens observed in the foliage
blends in the distance into one dark shade,
then changes to dark blue, which gradually fades
out to a hazy uncertainty where it is lost at the
sky-line.

As long ago as 1853, the variety and abundance of the natural growth of fruits throughout the Ozarks was observed by Professor Swallow, who then advised the planting of vines.

Beyond the Wilderness is the Marble Cave
property and the entrance to the Cave is through
a large sink-hole in the top of Roark Mountain.
This hole is said to be about two hundred feet
long, one hundred feet wide and thirty-five feet
deep. It is shaped like a great oblong bowl
with sloping sides, divided irregularly near the
middle, and having the bottom broken out in a
jagged way that is very handsome and gives
an ample support to the growth of ferns, wild

roses, and other vegetation with which it is abundantly decorated. About half of the descent into the basin is accomplished by scrambling down the roughly broken rocks, and the balance by a broad wooden stairway ending at a narrow platform that supports the locked gate.

For kind and valuable assistance rendered to insure the success and pleasure of the visit to the wonderful cave, which they regard with affection and pride, very cordial thanks are due to Capt. T. S. Powell, former manager, his son, Mr. Will Powell, the first guide, and Mr. Fred Prince, who has made the only official survey and map. It may be stated here that the survey and map are far from complete, and many known passages have never yet been entered.

Being the first visiting party of the season, certain disadvantages were encountered in a great accumulation of wet clay and rubbish, washed in by the rains since the previous summer; but the gate was opened with considerable effort, and slowly and cautiously we descended the slippery, clay-banked stairs to the immense mound of debris forty-five feet below the gate, to behold, at last, the grandeur of the Auditorium.

The magnificence of that one chamber should give to Marble Cave a world-wide fame even if there were nothing more beyond. The blue-gray

limestone walls have a greater charm than those
of an open cañon, owing to the fact that they
sweep away from any given point in long, true
curves to form an elliptical chamber three
hundred and fifty feet long by one hundred and
twenty-five feet wide, with the vault above
showing absolute perfection of arch, and measuring, by the survey, from its lowest to its
highest point, one hundred and ninety-five
feet. These measurements are said to be
indisputably correct, and if so, the Auditorium of
Marble Cave is the largest unsupported, perfect
arch in the world; it being one hundred feet
longer than the famous Mormon Tabernacle at
Salt Lake City. In addition to the artistic
superiority of architectural form, its acoustic
properties having been tested, it is found to be
truly an auditorium. The curving walls and
pure atmosphere combine to aid the voice, and
carry its softest tones with marvelous distinct-
ness to every portion of the immense inclosed
space. As a concert hall its capacity has been
tested by musicians who are said to have been
enthusiastic over the success of their experiments. Several years ago a piano was lowered
into the cave for use on a special occasion, and
still occupies a position on the dancing platform,
where it will probably remain indefinitely under
the scant protection of a small canvas tent.

The chief ornament of the Auditorium is the

White Throne, a stalagmitic mass that when
viewed from the stairway appears to rest solid-
ly against the most distant wall, and looks so
small an object in that vast space as to render a
realization of its actual measurement impossible.
The height of the Throne is sixty-five feet and
the girth two hundred. It is a mass of dripstone resting on a limestone base reserved from
the ancient excavation to receive it, and on careful inspection the perpendicular lines, observed
on the front, are found to be a set of rather large
organ pipes. A fresh fracture shows the Throne
to be a most beautiful white and gold onyx.
The outer surface has now received a thin coating of yellow clay which was, of course,
regretted, but later observations on onyx building reveals the pleasing fact that if the crystal-
bearing waters continue to drip, the yellow clay
will supply the coloring matter for a golden
band of crystal.

The Throne is hollow and has a natural opening in one side by which it may be entered, but
the space within is too limited to invite a
lengthy stay. That portion of the outside
which is nearest the wall is formed with sufficient irregularity of outline to admit of an
ascent to the top, and the view obtained is well
worth the difficult scramble up and the appre-
hensive slide down. Being raised so high above
all objects that divide attention or in some

degree obstruct the view, permits a freedom of outlook that sensibly increases the appreciation of the vastness of the enclosed chamber and its enclosing walls. Efforts to establish the age of the deposit by observations on the yearly growth, would afford little satisfaction, for the obvious reason that conditions governing the growth are dependent, in a measure, on each season's vegetation. Deposit began, of course, after the erosion of the chamber ceased, and therefore represents only a fraction of the age of the cave itself. About thirty feet west of the White Throne and against the wall, stands the next onyx attraction in the form of a beautiful fluted column nearly twenty feet high, tapering up from a base three feet in diameter, and known as the Spring Room Sentinel, because the Spring of Youth is just behind it although not directly connected with the Auditorium; it being the first chamber on the left in Total Depravity Passage, a wet and dangerous way of which next to nothing is known, but the entrance to which is a fine arch a few feet west of the Sentinel. The Spring of Youth is reached by climbing through a window-like opening, and is very small, very wet, very cold, and very beautiful. It is not more than ten feet high nor six in its greatest length and breadth, but every inch of its irregular surface is composed of dripstone of a bright yellowish-red and colorless crystal; and

down the glittering walls trickles clear and
almost ice-cold water, to the onyx floor where it
is caught and held in a marvelous fluted bowl of
its own manufacture. This is said to be the
gem of the whole cave and seems to have been
placed where it is for the consolation of those
who are unable to enjoy the peculiar grandeur
of the Auditorium, and leave it as some actually
are said to do, with a sense of disappointment,
because it is not the gleaming white hall of
marble which some writers for reputable
journals have allowed their imaginations to
create.

In winter the Spring of Youth Room takes on
a complete coating of ice, with icicles of all
sizes hanging from the ceiling and projections.
The effect is described as being wonderfully
beautiful.

Further down Total Depravity Passage we
were not urged to go, because at that season of
the year it is wet and difficult, without any
sufficient promise of a brilliant compensation for
the achievement of such a journey. But the
Spring of Youth Room, or as it is generally
called, the Spring Room, is more than ample
justification for the existence of the passage,
and would still be if that passage were several
miles in length and the attraction located at the
most distant limit.

The various passages in Marble Cave are by

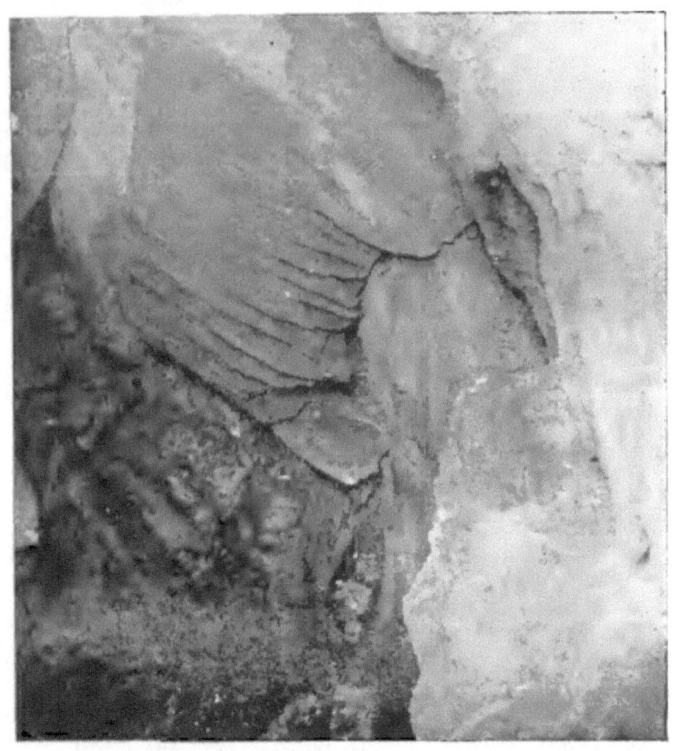

WALL IN SPRING ROOM.
Page 32.

no means alike or even similar; some having
been opened by the action of water assisted only
by acid carried in solution; while others are the
unmistakable crevices of earthquake origin,
afterwards enlarged, or perhaps only remodeled,
as we might say, by the water's untiring energy
in changing the position of rock masses without
obliterating evidences of original design.

A glance at the map shows the sudden breaking off of the various passages represented; the
end, however, is not of the passages themselves,
but only of the exploration or the survey of them,
and there is a possibility that future develop-
ments will lead to the discovery of more caves
than are yet known. However that may be, the
glimpses already had into the beyond are said
to be alluring.

To the north of the Auditorium, which was
until recently called the Grand Amphitheater,
there opens out a kind of alcove extension known
as the Mother Hubbard Room, and spreading
out from this is the corridor, a room about one
hundred and twenty-five feet long and seventy-
five feet in width, with a low, narrow passage,
or crawl, leading from the northeast into the
Grotto, a dome-shaped room formerly called the
Battery, on account of the great number of bats
that used to congregate in it. It is about forty
feet in diameter and fifty feet in height. On
one side of this room is a narrow "squeeze"

opening into a passage several feet lower than the floor level of the Grotto and leading to the Spanish Room, which when discovered bore indications of having been occupied by a human being who had tried to escape by tunneling, or by reaching a hole in the roof; which is said to be impossible for him to have done without outside assistance. As no bones have been found we may hope the assistance arrived in time. When the discovery of the room was made, a quantity of loose rock was piled before the entrance, so if he ever escaped it was not by that way.

After crawling back to the Corridor, through the same small, but dry passage of seventy feet length, we saw a narrow ledge of fine crystals, a deposit of Epsom salts, and a few bats that in the dim light looked white but are a light tan color with brown wings. A good specimen hanging on a projecting ledge of the wall remained undisturbed by us and our lights, giving an opportunity for careful inspection so that we presently discovered it to be a mummy; which naturally suggests that this portion of the cave, being dry and opening out of the great temple-like Auditorium as an alcove, could be converted into an imposing crypt.

Making our way across the room to its south-west extremity over a varied assortment of bowlders and down a drop of eight or ten feet,

we crawled into another tight-fitting dry passage
lined with beautiful glittering onyx like clear
ice banded with narrow lines of red, of which
broken fragments covered the narrow floor and
made a dazzling, but distressingly painful rug
to crawl over. This is the West Passage and
leads to the Grand Crevice, of which only a
small portion has been surveyed; midway of the
passage are the Epsom Rooms, two in number,
and well supplied with epsomite or native Epsom
salts; this is sometimes called the Windy Passage, on account of a rushing current of air met
suddenly at the first bend and, no doubt, due to
the meeting here of fresh air coming in from the
outside with that chemically changed in the
Epsom Rooms.

The cave contains a great many dangerous
places, as we correctly surmised on the morning
of our introduction; when Mr. Powell's blessing
on the breakfast was lost in so fervent a prayer
for the safe and successful accomplishment of
our undertaking, it seemed inconsiderate not to
present the reassuring appearance of inexhaust-
ible endurance.

In the Corridor can be seen one of the three
old Spanish ladders found in the cave when it
was rediscovered; but when and for what purpose the Spaniards used the cave there seems to
be no means of finding out. It should be
remembered that this part of the United States

was occupied first by the Spaniards and then by the French, and is a portion of the Louisiana Purchase, a tract of 897,931 square miles, or 70,000 square miles more than the original thirteen states. The price asked and paid was $12,000,000 and the assumption of claims which citizens of this country had against the French Government for about $3,750,000 more. The French offered to make the sale on account of being thoroughly discouraged with constant troubles arising with the Indians, whom they had decided it would be impossible to persuade or compel to recognize any laws other than those established by each tribe for itself, or accepted by friendly treaty with the council and disregarded by individuals on both sides:—and the United States accepted the offer, not for any expected value in the land, but for the unrestricted navigation of the Mississippi River. Therefore Missouri was never under British rule and never changed hands by force of arms.

But to return to the Spanish ladder, it is a tall pine tree notched on the sides for steps, and the stump of a branch left or a peg inserted at considerable intervals, for hand supports to assist in raising the weight of the body.

Returning to the Auditorium, we entered a passage behind the Great White Throne and started on what might well be called the Water Route, for no dry spot is touched on the round

trip; but if one goes prepared for such a journey it is well worth the effort and the mud.   If
the visitor is a man, the suit worn should be one
he is ready to part with, or overalls; ladies receive the same advice even to the overalls, as
some of the most beautiful portions of the cave,
which we failed to see, can be visited only in
that objectionable costume.   To visit any cave
comfortably a short dress is necessary and if
any thing like a thorough knowledge of the
ramifications is desired, the unavoidable climbing will soon prove the superior claims of a divided skirt; but if it is properly made, only the
wearer need be conscious of the divide.   Rub-
ber boots and water-proof protection for the
head and shoulders complete a costume that is
.not exactly an artistic creation, unless our
ideas of art have been gathered in the school of
Socrates, but it is suited to the requirements of
the occasion and makes the explorations far
more easy and profitable than they otherwise
could be.

The passage back of the White Throne is
called the Serpentine Passage, and most of it is
sufficiently high for traveling in an erect position; yet there are several places that require
crawling. The first stopping point is the Gulf
of Doom Room, or as it is also known, the Register Room, because here visitors usually write
their names in the peculiar dark red clay,

which is moist but firm and cuts with a polish.
This room is twenty-five feet high and fifty feet
wide, and looks off into the Gulf of Doom,
which seems rightly named when a rock is
thrown into it and you note the lapse of time
before any sound returns; and when the awful
Gulf is made visible by lights thrown in, one
involuntarily seeks a firmer footing and clings
to a projecting rock. The height of the Gulf
is ninety-five feet and the distant sound of falling water is not reassuring. The walls are not
smoothly worn away, but have the rough and
weird appearance of having been torn by a
torrent in a narrow mountain gorge, and are
stained with the dark clay.

Retracing our steps a short distance, if that
style of locomotion could be called steps, we
turned into Doré's Gallery, and surely that
artist was in his usual working mood when he
conceived this awful method of connecting the
upper regions with the lower. Great bowlders
have fallen down without helping to fill the
black holes that received them, and into this real
Inferno we proceeded to descend by narrow,
ladder-like stairs provided with a light hand rail,
and trembling slightly with the responsibility
they assumed. If any one's courage trembled
too, no notice was taken of it, and a record of
exploring experiences does not necessarily include
a confession of any doubts.

On all the ladders in this Gallery was a fine
white fungus growth in the form of a thick,
heavy mould, that the lightest touch destroyed.
In caves where some care is taken to protect
this mold, it attains a growth of six or more feet
and assumes the forms of sea-weed.

Once down the first and longest flight of
stairs, without any signs of a Doré dragon raising its huge body by heavy claws to a resting
place among the rocks, awe divides more evenly
with admiration; and being already well be-
smeared with mud, we climbed over the clay-
covered bowlders and crawled through narrow
holes with perfect satisfaction, enjoying each
novel scene to the utmost.

Off from the Doré Gallery is a small chamber
containing the Fountain of Youth, that must be
seen, but the way, like that of the transgressor,
is hard.   Arrived at the entrance we hesitated
a moment, for although getting in looked possible,
the way out again seemed not so simple; but
finally trusting to Providence, through the direct
agency of our careful guardians, of course, we
sat down on the edge of the large slippery
bowlder on which we stood, and reaching out
caught a projection of the wall on one side and
a bowlder crag on the other, swung off and
dropped into the soft mud below.   This chamber
proved to be a little gem; small but high, and
beautifully adorned with calcite crystal.   Down

a wall of red onyx on one side clear water flows
into a basin in the irregular, rocky floor, just
behind the bowlder we had used for a hand-rest
at the entrance; the perfectly transparent water
in the basin appears to be only a few inches deep,
but measures three feet, and is several degrees
colder than the air, which in this portion of the
cave is warm. The other wall of this room is
an almost perpendicular bank of the soft dark
red clay, in which small selenite crystals are
sprouting like plants in a garden.

Suddenly we heard a heavy, rolling noise like
distant thunder, and asking if it were possible
to hear a thunder storm so far below the surface,
were told it was the protest of angry bats against
a further advance on the quarters to which they
have retreated from the main body of the cave,
and their orders were obeyed: so of what may be in
that direction, we gained no positive knowledge
besides bats, and the fact that, small as they are,
their great numbers make them dangerous when
angry. Returning to the gallery and continuing
the journey down over slippery rock and
slender ladders we came at length to the bottom
of the Gulf of Doom, into which we had looked
from the room now high above us; and we
needed no stimulating help to the imagination to
pronounce it a fit termination to an artist's
troubled dream.

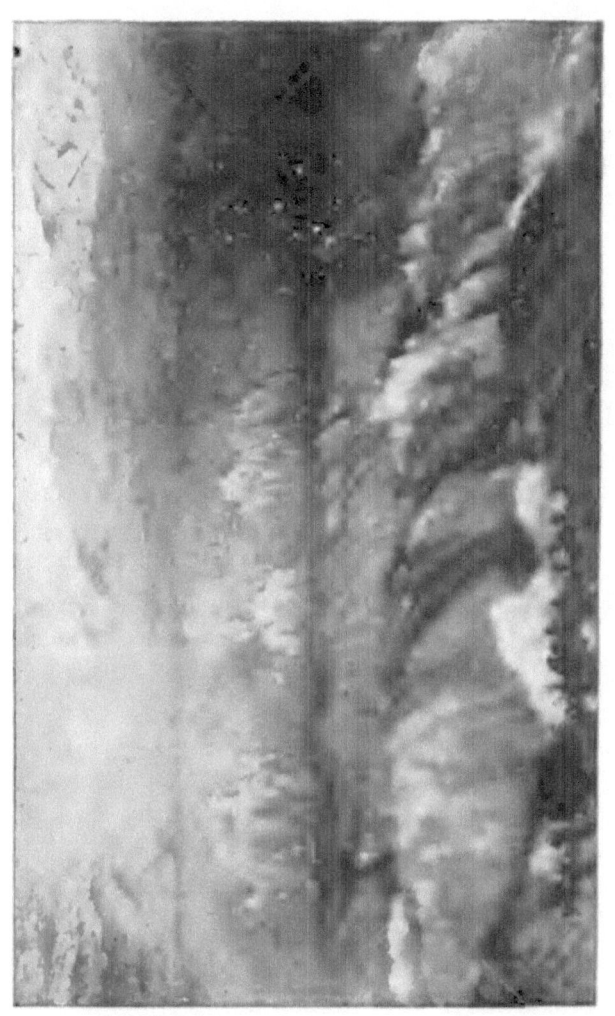

THE WATERFALL.

Page 41.

Then climbing over an assortment of bowlders of all sizes, going up a little, and swinging or sliding down, we came to a point in the narrow passage where the floor is a flat slab, like a large paving stone, tilted up at a steep angle against one wall and not reaching the other by about fifteen inches, with darkness of unknown depth below: about three feet above this opening the wall projects in a narrow, shelving ledge, and everything is covered with a thin coating of slippery wet clay. The only way to cross that uninviting bridge is to brace the feet against the slab, and leaning on the ledge, slowly work across. A little more rough work and the descent of the two short ladders, brought us, at last, under the beautiful Waterfall, where we stood as in a heavy shower of rain at the lowest point yet reached in the cave, which according to the survey of Mr. Prince is four hundred feet below the surface. The falling water has ornamented the walls, which in this portion of the cave expose over two hundred feet of Magnesian Limestone, with unique forms of dripstone; and the steeply sloping floor has received the over-charge of calcium carbonate until it has become a shining mass of onyx, retaining pools of cold, transparent water in the depressions. In the lowest corner there is only mud, and above it rises, to a height of at least fifteen feet a bank of miry, yellow clay, at the top of which a hole in the wall is the only known entrance to Blondy's Throne.

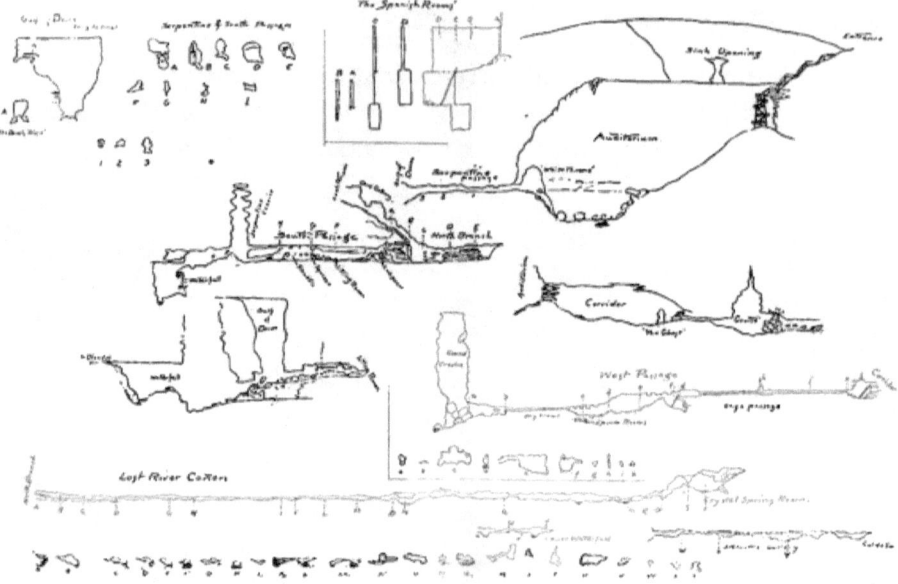

LONGITUDINAL AND CROSS-SECTIONS OF PASSAGES IN MARBLE CAVE, STONE CO., MISSOURI.

Plotted by Fred Prince, 1894.

CHAPTER III.

On account of the long "crawl" through mud and cold water, it was at first suggested and then strongly advised, that we should not undertake to make the trip to Blondy's Throne: and yearning to see what is considered the cave's chief beauty was not easy to over-come, but after careful attention to the deep mire of the approach the advice seemed good, especially as Mr. Powell kindly promised to write a description of its trials and treasures; which he promptly did, thereby making it possible for us to continue the journey now without a disappointing interruption, so we will proceed to wade that mud bank with him in his own way. He says: "As Mecca is to the Mohammedan, so is Blondy's Throne Room to the pilgrim who invades the chaos and penetrates the mysteries of Marble Cave. When the subject is mentioned to the guide, he shrugs his shoulders and assumes an imploring look, and begins at once to mention the difficulties of getting there. But if you insist upon it he will go. The passage by which this room has to be reached, if passage it may

43

be called, must be entered from the Waterfall Room, and a steep ascent must be made until an elevation of fifty feet is reached above the bottom of that room. This ascent has been called Hughse's Slide, as a man of that name once lost his footing at the top and slid on the wet and very slippery clay all the way to the bottom, leaving a very sleek trail. The ascent is difficult, as the soft clay is deep and wet and the sides are reeking and covered also with soft yielding clay. When the top of the slide is once reached, a low passage six feet wide and two feet high is discovered, and stooping low, or actually lying flat down, you enter. The top of the passage is of smooth rock and the bottom is of wet clay with an occasional variation of sharp gravel. The air is good, and as a lizard, you start forward. In places the passage widens to ten or twelve feet and again narrows to six feet.

"In about one hundred feet you encounter a small pond of water filling the whole width of the passage and extending twenty to thirty feet, but the guide tells you it is only one foot deep, and calls attention to the fact that the water does not come within a foot of the roof of the passage and you can easily keep your chin above it, and with this assurance through you go.

"Within the next one hundred feet you encounter and pass in the same manner three

more ponds of varying sizes. The guide calls
your attention to the fact that you are not alone,
and looking about you by the dim light of your
candle you see numbers of small eyeless salamanders, from four inches to one foot long. They
are peaceable and harmless, appear to have no
teeth and are easily caught, if you so desire.

"Another hundred feet and the Rest Room, or
Egyptian Temple is reached, and rising to your
feet you may rest. The room is small, but contains beautifully fluted walls, resembling basal-
tic columns; and natural marks of erosion that
resemble hieroglyphic inscriptions. From the
other side of this room the passage goes on with
the same characteristics, but as you enter to go
forward a sound strikes the ear, and you pause
to listen. It is a confusion of sounds, a babel
of voices; and sounds like a distant conversation
carried on by a large number of people. So
striking is this resemblance that you instantly
ask the guide if there are people in the room
ahead, and hardly believe him when he says,
'No.'

"You hear voices of men, voices of boys, babies,
girls and ladies, and occasionally loud laughter;
but forward is the word and on you go, encour-
aged by the assurance of the guide that you are
now over half way through the passage and that
the sounds came from Blondy's Throne Room.
Suddenly the passage divides into two much

alike, and taking the right hand one, you make
your slow advance until at last, with clothes
soaked and covered with clay mud, and your
strength about gone, you begin to feel desperate
and tell the guide that you will go no further,
when you see him rise to his feet, and he says :
' Here we are.' You step over a steep bank of
clay and emerge into a large room. It is almost
square in shape; about eighty feet long and sixty
feet wide, and about fifty feet high, with
white, smooth walls and a pure white ceiling,
and sloping gradually downward on the left ends
in a small, clear lake of water. This lake has a
beautiful beach of white pebbles, and though
shallow on the edge seems quite deep at the
center; in fact it is believed to have there a
concealed opening that gives exit to its waters.
On the opposite side from you, a stream of clear
water pours into the lake, and in doing so it
gives off the sounds that in the passage you mis-
took for human voices; and this noble stream
has been named Mystic River. It enters the
lake from under a beautiful natural arch, about
thirty feet across at the bottom, and six feet
above the water at the center. The bed of the
stream is eroded from strata of sandstone that is
extremely hard, containing corundum, and so
perfect is its continuity that it conveys sound
distinctly for a distance far beyond the reach of
the human voice, when tapped upon with a

hammer. The top of the arch is studded with lovely stalactites, clear as glass, that extend to the outer edge of the arch and form massive and beautiful groups there. Above the arch is a large opening. In truth the side of the room is out, and a great dark space appears like a curtain of black. A natural path leads up over one side of the arch, and following the lead of the guide you go up above and learn that a room on the higher level extends off in that direction and gets larger and higher. The walls are stalagmitic columns in cream color and decked in places with blood-red spots or blotches of Titanic size. The ceiling you cannot see. It is too high for the lights you have to reach. On the left you are suddenly confronted by a stalagmitic formation so large and so grand that all others are dwarfed into insignificance. You think of the dome of the Capitol at Washington. You are standing at the sloping base but cannot see the top. Just here the guide announces in an awestruck voice "Blondy's Throne." And who is Blondy? Only a fair-haired, blue-eyed, intrepid and daring fifteen-year-old boy, named Charles Smallwood, who assisted the writer in exploring the cave in the early days of 1883, and going on in advance, reported back that he had found another and a greater throne than the Great White Throne in the Auditorium.

"Well, here we are at Blondy's Throne at last,

and surveying the base, we find that it is actually only half in the room we are in; the other half forms the side of another room. In a word, the Great Throne divides the room into two parts and makes two rooms of it instead of one. Yet the one half of the base has a measurement, by tape line, of one hundred and fifty feet. The guide now makes preparations to ascend the Throne. A chain has been fastened up towards the top, and by taking hold of this the climb can be made up the sloping sides of the Throne. We pass on and up over the clearest and most ice-like formation, resembling the great icebergs seen at sea. Reaching an elevation of sixty feet an opening into the dome is found, and stooping, you enter. It is a room about twenty feet across, with a white ice-like floor, a roof or ceiling ten feet above, and from it hang thousands of brilliant stalactites and from the floor stalagmites rise up to meet them. They are in all sizes, from an inch to two feet across. The sides are of the same material joined and cemented lightly together. Strike any of them and clear musical notes are given off; a musician has found two full octaves. Water is dripping in many places, and in the center of the floor is a tank full of clear water. It is four feet wide, twelve feet long and of unknown depth.

"On the opposite side of the room from which you enter there is a hole or opening in the wall,

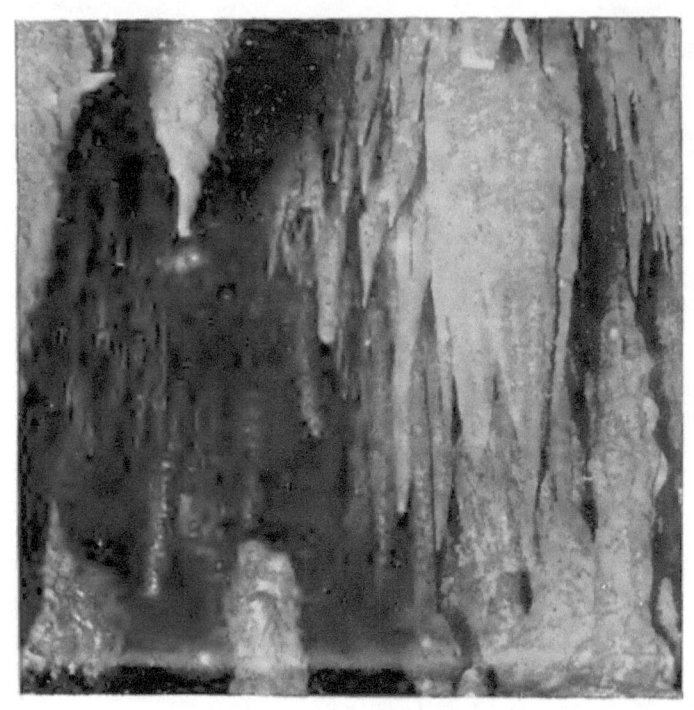

BLONDY'S THRONE.
Page 47.

It is large enough to go through but it goes into the great dark room on the other side of the Throne. An abyss confronts you, a sheer precipice which descends for many feet, perhaps hundreds. No man knows. This outer room of Blondy's Throne has been named the Chamber of the Fairies. Leaving it and continuing the ascent, the top of the Throne is soon reached and is about twenty feet across; and from several points still higher, rise stalagmitic spires.

"The actual height of Blondy's Throne is not known, but is probably about one hundred feet. Again look upwards for the ceiling from the dizzy height on top of the Throne; you cannot see it. Burn magnesium ribbon and look up, and you see a white ceiling spangled with groups of stalactites. It is surely one hundred feet away. Then look off into the unknown room which is called the Great Beyond. No human being has ever explored or even entered it, but fire balls thrown in reveal the fact that it is of great extent; and part of the bottom water and part land. No way of getting into it has ever yet been found, so its mysteries, lessons and revelations are still safe from human intrusion. How far it goes, where it stops, and what it leads to, are facts for some future explorer to discover. Bats and white salamanders are found in Blondy's Throne Room, and

some larger animals have been heard to jump
into the water and escape on the approach of
man, but their species is not known.

" The arched passage of Mystic River has been
followed up for a journey of an hour, but further than that its extent is unknown. It was
hoped that a way would be thus found into the
Great Beyond, but it did not prove successful.
A well equipped party could find there a chance
for some grand discoveries, and it would be one
of the notable pleasures of the life of the writer
to be one of such a party.

"The exit from Blondy's Throne Room is always made with deep regret that the waning
lights and meager supplies will not allow a longer stay. The long crawl, the mud and the water are all forgotten, and notwithstanding the
terror of the trip one feels well repaid."

We thank Mr. Powell for a charming journey
without its discomfort and danger, and re-
sume our travels at the Waterfall.

From the foot of the Waterfall we returned
again to the Auditorium, in time to enjoy a
sight such as we supposed could exist only in a
brilliant imagination; and the return at that
hour was not a lucky accident of fate, but the
result of careful attention to a prearranged design that we should not fail to witness a marvelous display never surpassed by lavish Na-

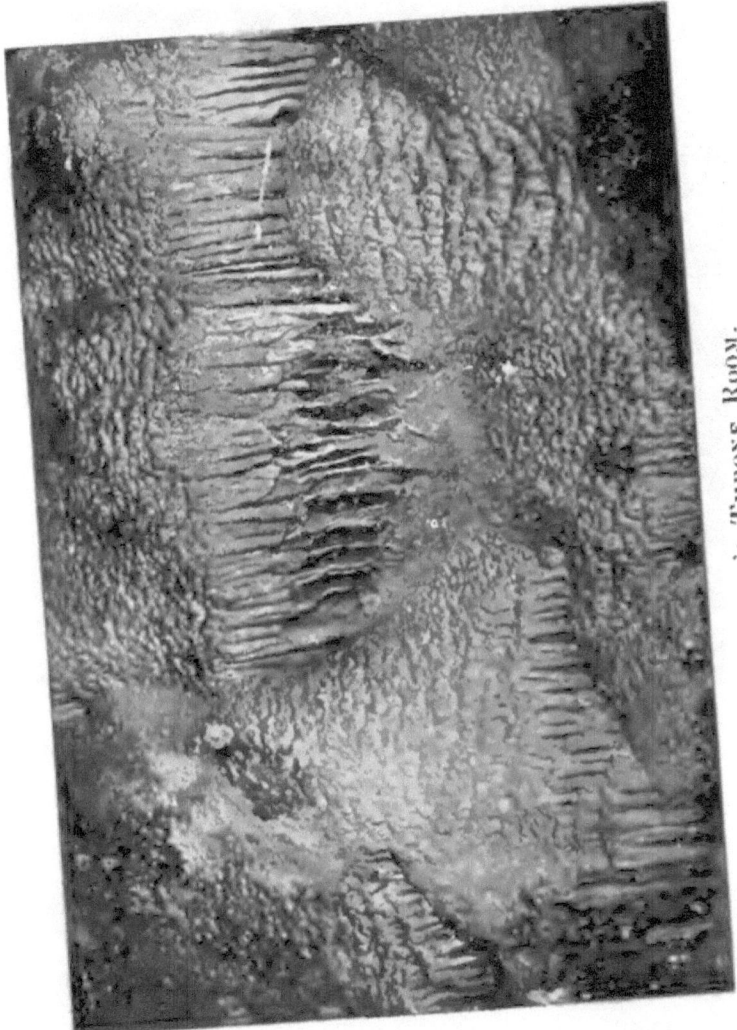

BLONDY'S THRONE ROOM.
Page 50.

FOOT OF WATERFALL.
Page 50.

ture. The day outside was one of cloudless summer sunshine.

Our eyes having grown accustomed to the dim light of candles in passages where absolute darkness, unrelieved by the stars of midnight, always reigns, the great Auditorium appeared before us softly flooded with daylight diffused from a broad white beam slanting down in long straight lines from the entrance as from a rift in heavy clouds; only this rift displayed around its edges a brilliant border of vegetation that the rough rocks cherish with tender care.

As we stood lost in almost speechless admiration, and without the slightest warning of treasure yet in store, the white beam was stabbed by a narrow, gleaming shaft of yellow sunlight. The glorious, radiant beauty of the picture presented is utterly indescribable, but it was of short duration, and in a few seconds the golden blade was withdrawn as suddenly as it had appeared.

If the genius of Elkins had been granted the privilege we enjoyed, the artist-world of Europe that graciously yielded the highest honor to his "Sunbeam on Mount Shasta," would have knelt in rapturous humility. Speaking of his great work, as we stood before it only a few months before his death, Mr. Elkins said quietly: "It is no great achievement; I simply painted it exactly as it looked. Anyone could do the same." But no one ever has.

The white beam was more enduring and by its aid we were able to view the expanse of the great Auditorium far better than could have been done in the momentary glare of any brilliant artificial light. Every part of the cloud-gray walls shows a stratification as regularly horizontal as if the laying of each course had been done with the assistance of line and level; while in every direction are now seen hundreds of stalactites that had not been noticed before, and although they look small, the average length, taken with the surveying instruments, is fourteen feet. The Hill beneath the entrance is an accumulation of debris, drifted in from the outside, and rising to a height of more than one hundred and twenty-five feet; while the great circumference of its supporting base, revealed by the banishment of shadows, suggests the possibility of tragic history of which the only evidence lies buried there and may or may not ever be discovered; but let us step lightly, since our feet may press the covering that shields a final sleep; and also let a grieving sister in her old age take comfort in the knowledge that here, as in few other spots, nature provides a certain and gentle burial for the unfortunate, and for a few seconds each day lights the dim chamber with a heavenly glory—perhaps in appeal to the sons of one country to harbor no such feelings as deprived Abel of life and for all time and eternity tarnished the honor of Cain.

The chilliness presently recalled us from further indulgence in that great scene, to ordinary affairs; and consulting the reliable thermometer, it was found to register 42°, while in some of the lower passages the temperature is 58°; but the variation is not in accordance with the accepted theory of one degree to the one hundred feet descent.

A return to the beautiful Spring of Youth Room was now a necessity, but we were careful to allow no drop of water falling from clay-stained hands to reach the purity of that lovely bowl, and then being happy and hungry, we retired to the piano's protecting tent for refreshment.

The atmosphere in Marble Cave has the peculiar bracing and invigorating quality common to the majority of caves, that seems almost to defy fatigue and encourage exertion that under ordinary conditions would be impossible.

After the exertion necessary in the warmer portions of the cave, the temperature of 42° proved rather low for comfort and finally was admitted to be a sufficient reason for either leaving the cave or sending out for the wraps. Slowly and reluctantly the party walked up the

long winding path to the summit of the Hill
where the stairway finds support, stopping
many times to admire again the perfect curves
and fine color-tones of that wonderful high
arch—within a mountain yet softly radiant with
the light of day.

Still lingering regretfully among the fern-
decked rocks before quite finishing the ascent to
the actual outside world, the mercury lost little
time in registering eighty degrees.

Since no official, or even approximately correct map of Marble Cave has yet been published,
and the desirability of maps is particularly urged by Monsieur E. A. Martel, a special effort was
made to secure one, which was accompanied by
the following remarks from Mr. Prince in regard
to its incompleteness:

"There are several passages and rooms which
do not appear on the map, though some of them
are well known, but have not been surveyed and
platted.

"Much further exploration is possible in this
great cavern. Lost River Canon ends abruptly
in a bank of red clay, the volume of water being
undiminished. The water from the Great Fall
flows by a small serpentine into a passage which
has never been followed up; its entrance being
several hundred feet higher that the nearest
water level."

Unfortunately the quantity of water in the

cave at the time of the visit just described was so unusually great as to render the Lost River Canon trip impossible.

During the previous season the cave and its surroundings were visited by a prominent naturalist who appears to have been delightfully liberal in the diffusion of scientific knowledge and the explanations of methods of pursuing investigations. His practical instruction in snake catching is particularly interesting as it was never before introduced into this state, where the copperhead and rattler are known to have survived among the fittest. Seeing a snake hole and desiring information as to the family record of the proprietor, he inserted a finger, and while waiting for results explained that there is no better way to secure a specimen, as the enraged reptile will fasten its fangs into the intruding member and then can be easily withdrawn. It is a pleasure to state that even snakes recognize the claims of friendship, and no injury was experienced. *

In the vicinity of Marble Cave there are several choice varieties of onyx and marble, among them a rare and beautiful onyx in black and yellow. The coloring, tinting and banding of onyx seem generally to be regarded as one of the unexplainable mysteries of nature, but is in

* The naturalist referred to is the late Prof. E. D. Cope.

reality an extremely simple process that can be
easily studied in any active cave.

When the percolating acidulated water passes
slowly through a pure limestone it is filtered of
impurities and deposits a crystal, either pure
white or transparent; if it comes in contact
with metallic bodies of any kind, it carries
away more or less in solution to act as coloring
matter; the beautiful pale green onyx in several Missouri counties taking its tint from the
copper; in South Dakota, manganese in various
combinations produces black and many shades
of brown; in both states an excessive flow of
water often carries a quantity of red or yellow
clay which temporarily destroys the beauty of
exposed surfaces, but in after years becomes a
fine band of brilliant color.

Small wind caves are numerous in the Ozarks
and being cold are frequently utilized for the
preservation of domestic supplies. The entrance
to one in the neighborhood of Marble Cave is
high up on the hillside south of Mr. Powell's
house and being visible from the porch was too
tempting to be ignored, and the walk up to it
for a better view was rewarded with a most
charming bit of scenery as well. All the quiet
valley, divided by a rushing little stream, lay
before us in the shadow of early evening, while
to the north and east the hills were brilliant in
summer sunshine, with one small open glade

ENTRANCE TO CAVE—INTERIOR VIEW.
Page 52.

gleaming vividly among the darker shades of forest green.

The cave was a very small room at the bottom of a steep, rocky, sloping passage, and contained no standing water, although there had been a heavy rainfall the night before and the opening is so situated as to especially favor the inflow, which naturally indicates a greater cave beneath a hidden passage. Here, as in most of the caves of the region, is found a small lizard: it is totally blind but its ancestors evidently were not, as is shown by conspicuous protuberances where the eyes should be, but over which the skin is drawn without a wrinkle or seam to indicate a former opening. These harmless creatures are not scaly, but are clothed in a soft, shining, well-fitted skin, and the largest seen were little more than six inches long.

Those who love perfect Nature in a most smiling mood should hasten to visit Marble Cave while yet no rail-road quite touches the county.

CHAPER IV.

Fairy Cave enjoys the reputation of being the most beautiful yet discovered in that cavernous region, and consequently a visit to it was contemplated with considerable eagerness, although the mode of entrance had been described with sufficient accuracy to prevent any misconception of the difficulties to be overcome or the personal risk involved. To go from our temporary abiding place it was necessary to pass Marble Cave, and when we had gone that far Mr. Powell left us to follow the road, while he, on his mule, took a short cut across the hills and valleys, to try to find men not too much occupied with their own affairs on a fine Monday morning, in corn plowing time, to join our expedition. As neither our small companion, Merle, nor ourselves, had any knowledge of the locality of our destination, we were carefully instructed to follow the main road to the Wilderness Ridge, and keeping to that, pass the Indian Creek road and all others that are plain, but turn down the second dim road and follow it until stopped by a new fence where we would be met and conducted. So long as points to be passed held out, these directions gave us no trouble whatever, even the first dim road offering no obstacle to the pleasure of our progress; but the second dim road proved so elusive we traveled many miles in search of it, finally bringing up against a place Merle was familiar with and knew to be a long way off the track of our intentions. As there was nothing to be done but return we naturally accepted the situation and did that; presently finding Mr. Powell and the Messrs Irwin, on whose land the cave is, patiently waiting for us in what was really not a road at all, but rather, in this region of fossils, the badly preserved impression of one long since extinct.

The new fence was opened at two places that we might drive through and be saved the exertion of walking a considerable distance, then the horses were left in the shade while we scrambled down the steep hill-side covered with sharp-edged, broken rock, about mid-way down which is the mouth of the cave, yawning like a narrow, open well. Above this a stout windlass has been arranged on two forked logs.

A few feet below the surface the cave spreads out jug-shaped, so that in descending nothing is touched until the floor is reached, one hundred feet beneath the surface; consequently the only danger to be apprehended is a fall.

Each of the three men present kindly offered to go down and make the exploration with me, but that would have left only two at the windlass, and for a man's weight, safety requires four. Should an accident occur, assistance would be necessary, and some time lost in finding it; so, to the undisguised satisfaction of one and equally evident relief of the others, it was reluctantly decided that the trip must be given up, and therefore we are indebted to the kindness of Captain Powell* for the following description of Fairy Cave:

"The Cave referred to is situated in Section 24, Township 23, Range 23, in Stone County, Missouri, and is on the homestead of one of three brothers named Irwin.

"It was accidentally discovered in the year 1895 and up to the time of this writing (June 1896) only six persons have ever entered it. It is in a point or spur of the Ozark Mountains which runs to the east from the great Wilderness Ridge, and is three miles distant from the Marble Cave. Having been one of the first to enter the Cave, being called by the owner as a sort of cave expert, I will attempt to describe both the adventure and the cave just as they were. The measurements are simply estimated, though by long practice I have become expert in that line also,

*Editor of the county news-paper.

but the longest measurement here was correctly taken by the rope used.

"Having been invited by the Irwin brothers to come and examine and explore a new cave they had found but had only entered and not explored, accompanied by my eldest son, W. T. Powell, I reached the place one warm Saturday morning. We found about twelve or fourteen men waiting for our coming; some discussing the matter of whether we would enter when we did come, and others who had volunteered to work the windlass, which had been erected over the opening, by means of which, with a one hundred foot rope, entrance was to be made. The opening was like a small well, and situated under the edge of an overhanging cliff of marble, and on the southeast slope of the mountain, about one hundred and fifty feet above the bottom of a narrow valley, and about the same distance below the top of the mountain, which here is three hundred feet high. In order to rig a windlass the edge of the cliff had to be broken away. The well-like opening descended for about ten feet through strata of flat-laying rocks that formed a roof; then all appeared to be vacancy and a stone cast in gave back a distant sound.

"Having first tested the air and proved it good by dropping in blazing excelsior saturated with turpentine, a stout oak stick was attached to the end of the rope, my son sprang astride and was lowered to the bottom, just one hundred feet. He reported back 'All right.' On the return of the rope I took my position on the stick and was soon dangling in mid air. The sensation was strange and exhilarating. Looking up I could only see the small opening I came through, and a straggling stream of light poured down that, but on all sides profound darkness reigned supreme. A spark-like light my son lit, reminded me of the lost Pleiad. About twenty-five or thirty feet from the top I caught sight of a scene that made me call on the men at the windlass to stop.

"This caused them to think something was going wrong and one called out to know what was the matter : I heard him say 'He is weakening.' I assured them everything was right only I wanted to take a view; so they stopped. Off at a distance of perhaps twenty-five feet was an opening about ten feet or more wide and twelve feet high. The light from the opening struck it fairly, owing to the position of the sun at the time. Through this opening I saw into another room, large and magnificent. It brought to mind the White City. It was snowy white, and thickly studded with stalactites and stalagmites of immense size and in great numbers; some looking like spires of numerous churches, and many connected as with a lattice-work about the bottom. For a short time I gazed on that lovely scene, and examined the chances to reach it, but a great gulf intervened that we had no means of spanning, and I called to the men to lower me down. Approaching the bottom one of the walls trended in towards me and I stepped upon solid ground close to the wall, which half way up seemed fifty feet away. The opening above now looked like a small pale moon, and the next man who came dangling down to join us looked no bigger than a toy soldier. Gradually our eyes became accustomed to the twilight, and by the time our party was increased to six men, I could see quite distinctly.

"The room runs directly into the mountain and is about ninety feet high, and where we landed it proved to be twenty feet wide. It extended in both directions, but much the farthest towards the right hand. The outer room is encrusted in fine white water formations. It forms a Gothic ceiling from which hang pendant at all places brilliant and sparkling stalactites; some being of immense size and length, from ten to twenty-five feet. Others are not so large but are brilliant. We created a flood of artificial light with dozens of candles and lamps; and then and not until then, could we see the slope and contour of the roof. A few bats were flitting about, disturbed for the first time. To the left, a vast white pillar extended from floor to roof. It was pure white and about five feet in diameter all

the way up. It was fluted, fretted, draped and
spangled. I never in my life saw anything more
chaste and lovely. I thought of the countless
ages it must have taken to form that monument:
of the streams of clear water that had fallen and
left their calcite deposits, while it grew year
after year, age after age, century after century,
in this profound darkness, disturbed by no noises
save the rhythmic sound of the falling drops and
the dull flitting of the bats, who alone were the
living witnesses of its construction. To the rear
of this great pillar the room is divided into
three galleries, one above another. With great
difficulty and much danger we climbed into each
of these. The floors were all like the pillar of
pure white onyx, and extended back a distance
of thirty or more feet. The floor of one formed
the roof of another. They were brilliant with
hanging pendants and the side walls were all
veneered with the same white and crystalline
formation. To entirely describe them is impossible. A day in each would still leave the
observer short of words in which to tell of the
wonders.

"Turning towards the right hand from the
entrance we advance two hundred feet up an
incline of dry clay, the room widening gradually
until its width is forty feet, when we reach the
top of an elevation thirty feet above the starting
point, where a sudden steep descent brings us to

a halt.   A stone cast down strikes water and the
sound of a splash comes back to us. With
caution we seek our way down the hill and stand
on the edge of a small lake or pond. Suddenly
my son, who is in the lead, rushes back saying:
'Look out! I put my hand on a snake.' Some
of us, being armed with hickory canes that had
been thrown down, concentrated our lights and
advanced.   Sure enough, there is a snake a yard
long coiled up on a section of rotten wood.   It
proves to be a copperhead, the most quarrelsome
and vicious snake in this country; but his nature
is changed so that he makes no effort to fight
and is killed with a blow, and is sent to be
hoisted up that we may examine him in daylight.
No others were found, and probably he had
fallen in at the opening, and spent a long, weary
time in expiation of his upper-earth crimes.

"Examining the lake we find it to be about
forty feet wide and the same long, and it fills
the room from wall to wall. We cannot pass it
so must either stop or wade through. We decide
to wade, and on measuring the water find it only
two or three feet deep, with a soft clay bottom,
and in many places islands of stalagmite rise
above the surface.

"On the sides of the lake there are formations
in the shape of sofas and lounges, and they appear to be cushioned, but the cushions are found
to be hard, solid rock. As the lights advance

across the lake new wonders are revealed.
Curtains and draperies hanging from the top
almost touch the water and entirely cut off the
view beyond.   Passing under a curtain at one of
the highest places, we emerge from the lake, and
once more on dry land, advance up a slope.
Here the water formations have taken human
shapes of all sizes and several colors now appear
and help to present a chaos of beauty.

"Two hundred feet more and the chamber ends
in a vast waterfall, but the water has turned to
stone.   Above the waterfall is an opening, but
it is twenty-five feet up a smooth wall and we
have no ladder.   The journey was at an end.
Tired, wet and muddy, we started on our return
trip ; recrossed the dark lake, and retraced our
steps to the place under the opening without
realizing that we had spent six hours under
ground.   While the other members of the party,
and the specimens, were being raised to the surface, the writer sought to learn the flora and
fauna of this new region.   The flora is blank.
Even the white mold so common in many caves
is absent; and no fungus grows on the poles,
bark and rotten wood that have at some past
time been cast in.

"In animal life the range is greater.   I have
mentioned the ever-present bats, and dozens of
them were seen.   There were also small, white
eyeless salamanders, small, yellow, speckled sal-

amanders, with signs of eyes but no sight; also a jet black salamander, which like the rest, was blind. The bats were of two species—the common brown bat and the larger light grey or yellow species. But this was not the time of the year to see many bats in caves. In the summer season most of them go out and remain until cool weather, and then return to the caves with their young; so I was rather surprised to see as many as we did.

"Down comes the rope for the last time, and taking my place, I soon feel myself spinning around and slowly rising. As I again pass the magic city I saw going down, a stronger wish than ever takes possession of me to go there, and I look for any chance to solve the problem of how such a journey can be made. ' Thou art so near and yet so far.'

"Suddenly I find myself emerging from the ground into a very hot world, with the evening sun blazing so that the air feels like the scorching heat of an oven; and my late companions are scattered about under the trees, no doubt wishing themselves back in the cool regions below the hot cliffs.

"My final conclusions in regard to Fairy Cave were that it was about six hundred feet long by from fifteen to forty feet wide and from eighty to ninety feet high: that in the upper story there are rooms that I could not reach, that will

amply pay the scientist and explorer to investi-
gate in the future: that probably we reached all
the accessible parts in the level we traveled :
that the temperature was fifty-six or very near
that degree: that small as it is, it contains the
finest formations and grandest scenery I have
ever seen in a cave: and I have examined over
one hundred of various sizes. I believe that for
interior beauty its equal is not to be found in
America , and I sincererely believe that the ver-
dict of future exploration will establish the truth
of the assertion, but as equally good judges
differ on such matters, time will be required for
atrue and just decision. There are yet many promising caves to be explored in this region, and if
my strength holds out a few years I hope to see
them all.   T. S. POWELL.''

POWELL CAVE.

As a measure of consolation for the disappointment of not seeing the beauty of Fairy
Cave, Mr. Irwin suggested that only a quarter
of a mile further on was another, recently discovered and worthy of a visit, although small.

In that region of steep hills and sharp-edged
rocks, a great amount of travel can be added to
the experience of a tender-foot in a short distance.
The quarter of a mile seemed to stretch out in
some mysterious way as we worked on it, but
the variety and abundance of attractions are
more than ample compensation.

The view was fine, including as it did the deep ravine and grassy, wooded slopes rising three hundred feet above, with here and there a handsome ledge of marble exposed like the nearly buried ruin of a forgotten temple of some past age. Scattered about in great profusion among the broken rock on the surface of these hill-sides we observed a water deposit of iron ore. It is a brown hematite and in some cases shows the structure of the bits of wood it has replaced. Since this region has from the earliest time produced a generous growth of vegetation, the decay of which has yielded a never-failing supply of acids to assist in carving the caves and then in their decoration, the presence of the ore is not difficult to account for. The whole Ozark uplift being rich in iron, the acidulated drainage waters coming into contact dissolved and took it in solution, to re-deposit where and when conditions should be favorable. These conditions were found in the basin among the hills and along its outlet.

In the Popular Science Monthly of January 1897, a short article by J. T. Donald, entitled "A Curious Canadian Iron Mine," describes the same thing going on at the present time in Lac a la Tortue, a small body of water in the center of a tract of swamp land, which produces the vegetation necessary to supply the acid required for a base of operation.

Of the manner of deposition he says: "The solution of iron in vegetable acid (in which the iron is in what the chemist calls the form of a protosalt) is oxidized by the action of the air on the surface of the lake into a persalt, which is insoluble, and appears on the surface in patches that display the peculiar iridescence character-istic of petroleum floating on water. Indeed, not infrequently these films of peroxide of iron are incorrectly attributed to petroleum. These films become heavy by addition of new particles; they sink through the water, and in this manner, in time, a large amount of iron ore is deposited on the lake bottom. It must not be supposed that the ore is deposited as a fine mud or sedi-ment. On the contrary, in this lake ore, as it is called, we have an excellent illustration of what is called concretionary action—that is, the tendency of matter when in a fine state of divi-sion to aggregate its particles into masses about some central nucleus, which may be a fragment of sunken wood, a grain of sand, or indeed a pre-formed small mass of itself."

It is claimed for this water ore, which is gathered like oysters, that mixed with bog ore and magnetic iron, and smelted with charcoal, the result as obtained is strong, durable and high priced.

The curiously elastic quarter of a mile finally yielded to persistent toil, and the cave was reached. The entrance is sufficiently broad to give a good first impression, and is under a heavy ledge of limestone which breaks the slope of the hill and is artistically decorated with a choice collection of foliage, among which is a coral honeysuckle; the fragrant variety grows everywhere. Under the ledge is a narrow vestibule, out of the north end of which is a passage about twenty-four inches in width, between perpendicular walls, and as steeply inclined as the average dwelling-house stairway but without any assisting depressions to serve as steps. Mr. Irwin cut a grape vine, and making one end secure at the entrance, provided a hand rail, by the aid of which I was able to easily descend the stepless way and afterwards remount.

The first chamber entered is the principal portion of the cave, and by actual measurement is forty-nine feet in length by forty-eight in greatest width and the height estimated at fifty feet. On account of irregularities it appears smaller but higher. On opposite sides of the chamber, at elevation about midway between the floor and ceiling are two open galleries. The floor is extremely irregular with its accumulation of fallen masses of rock, and the action of water has given to portions of the walls the appearance of pillars supporting the arches of the roof. The whole aspect is that of a small Gothic chapel. Off to the northwest is another room

measuring thirty feet in each direction, and out
of this are several openings, too small to squeeze
through, which indicate the possible existence
of other chambers beyond, but they may be only
drain pipes.

The cave contains no drip formations, notwithstanding which it is one of the most charming,
and when invited to name it I called it Powell
Cave, in honor of the most ardent admirer of
caves in that county, and to whom I am much
indebted for valued assistance.

CHAPTER V.

GENTRY CAVE.

The cave nearest to Galena, and the first visited by us, is Gentry Cave, situated a mile and a half from town. We started in the mail coach, but that vehicle met with a misfortune by no means unusual in that region, the total wreck of a wheel. Having only that morning arrived from the rich agricultural portion of the State where no surface rock can be found, we were pleased enough with the prospect of a walk in such charming spring weather, and set out with a cheerful certainty that the rough place in the road would soon be passed. But the school of experience is always open for the reception of new-comers and we were admitted to full duty without question.

The topography was nearly as broken, in its way, as the natural "piking" spread over it, and very beautiful with the dense forests lighted by the slanting yellow rays of the afternoon sun. The way leads up to the "ridge road" which is at length abandoned for no road at all, and

descending through the forest, more than half
the distance down to the James River flowing at
the base of the hill, we come suddenly in view
of the cave entrance, which is probably one of
the most magnificent pieces of natural architecture ever seen.

Rounding a corner by a narrow path, we step
onto a covered portico ninety-seven feet long,
with an average width of ten feet. The floor is
smooth and level, as also is the ceiling, which
is nine feet above, supported by handsomely
carved pillars and rising in a gray cliff projecting from the slope of the hill above, out to the
brink of the more abrupt descent to the water's
edge ninety feet below. Between the pillars
are three large door-ways into the cave. The
comparison suggested is an Egyptian temple,
and the idea is continued within, where there
are no chambers as in other caves; but instead,
the entire interior is a labyrinth of passages
winding about in every direction among an
uncounted number of low massive pillars, some
supporting a low ceiling and others connected
by high arches, the highest point being estimated at sixty feet, but appearing to be more,
because the enclosed space rising to a dome is so
narrow that the point of view is necessarily
directly underneath.   ·

All exposed surfaces of pillars and walls inside
the cave are of clay or a soft porous rock having

the same appearance, and are covered with curious little raised markings like the indescribable designs of mixed nothing generally known as "Persian patterns." This is, of course, easily explained; the clay being the residuum from disintegrated limestone, the markings described are the harder portions of the rock remaining after particles of clay had been carried out by flowing water while the disintegrating process was yet incomplete.

The Drinking Fountain is considered the great attraction of the cave, and appears to have been fashioned to suggest a model for the handsome soda fountains belonging to a later period. The water bowl is a large depression worn in the top of a rock which seems to have been built into the wall. In front it is five feet high and nine feet across, with artistic corners approximately alike, and at the back ornamental carving extends upward towards the ceiling with an opening through the wall at the center. This opening is divided by a short column down which water trickles to supply the bowl. The ceiling here is about thirty-five feet high and most of the exposed surface is a blue-gray limestone. Only one portion of Gentry Cave has received a deposit of dripstone and even that is of limited extent, and located at the end of a narrow slippery passage between high, slippery walls.

The fine entrance is of grey limestone in undisturbed horizontal strata, and this is so plainly
marked in the roof-supporting pillars as to give
them the appearance of having been prepared by
skillful hands, in several blocks, and afterwards
arranged in place without the aid of mortar.
Unfortunately, all efforts to photograph this
wonderful portico have failed to give satisfaction—its position above the river being such as
to afford no point for the proper placing of the
camera; but a second visit made for the purpose
of trying was far from being a loss, and part
of the reward consisted of finding among the
sheltered rocks, scarcely three feet above the
floor, two humming birds' nests with their
treasure of small eggs, and our little companion
who discovered them was pleased to leave them
untouched.

SUGAR TREE HOLLOW CAVE.

The name of this cave is due to the fact that
the approach is through a "hollow" well wooded
with sugar maple trees. It is two miles from
Galena and the drive a beautiful one, as much
of the way is through the forest without a road,
but with a charming little rushing, crooked
stream of clear, cold water: and in places the
green slopes give way to mural bluffs of grey
limestone in undisturbed strata.

The entrance to the cave is through a hole

about two feet high by three in width, into which we went feet first and wiggled slowly down an incline covered with broken rock, for a distance of fifteen feet, where a standing depth is reached. A flat, straight, level ceiling extends over the whole cave without any perceptible variation, and this is bordered around its entire length and breadth with a heavy cornice of dripstone, made very ornamental by the forms it assumes, and the multitude of depending stalactites that fall as a fringe around the walls. The line of contact between the cornice and ceiling is as clear and strong as if both had been finished separately before the cornice was put in place by skillful hands.

Dripstone covers the walls, which vary in height from one foot to twenty feet, according to the irregularities of the floor, just as the width of this one-room cave varies with the curves of the walls, which are sweeping and graceful, the average being twenty-nine feet, but is much greater at the entrance where the entire slope extends out beyond the body of the cave. The length, from north to south, measures two hundred and thirty-three feet exclusive of an inaccessible extension.

The south end of the cave rises by a steep slope to within a foot of the ceiling with which it is connected by short but heavy columns of dripstone, and another line of pillars of graduated height meets this at right angles near the middle and ends in an immense stalagmite that stands at the foot of the slope like a grand newel post.

There is no standing water in the cave, but everything is wet with drip, and consequently the formation of onyx is actively progressing and the south slope already mentioned shows a curious succession of changes in cave affairs. By the slow action of acidulated waters, the grey limestone deteriorated into a yellowish clay-bank, and now its particles are being re-united into solid rock by the deposit of calcium carbonate from the drip.

A careful test of the temperature of the atmosphere showed it to be fifty-eight degrees.

PINE RUN CAVE.

This also is a small cave easily visited from Galena, being less than two miles distant on the Marionville road. The entrance faces the road and is on the same level, consequently it is one of the easiest to visit. Just within is seen an opening in the ceiling, which we are told is one of the two ways to an upper chamber whose chief attraction is a dripstone piano, and the means of ascending is at hand in the form of a Spanish ladder; but an attempt of that sort might even cause the new woman to hesitate, and who hesitates is lost. The ascent was not

made. We advanced on a level with the road
for a distance of perhaps twenty feet, when the
direction of the cave changed with a right an-
gular turn and we were in a straight gallery
about two hundred and fifty feet long and
fifteen feet in width, the height gradually decreasing to about three feet towards the upper
end, where it widened out into a low but broad
chamber. The floor of this chamber is most
beautiful. It is composed of a series of connected calcite bowls whose beautifully fluted
rims are of regular and uniform height, and all
are equally filled with clear, still water. A
great number of these basins are said to have
been destroyed by an ax in the hands of a poor
witless creature for the gratification of a burst
of temper, and a magnificent stalagmitic column,
too heavy for one man to lift, lay detached and
broken, in proof that his body did not share the
feebleness of his mind.

Beyond these basins is a low passage through
which is found the second entrance to the upper
chamber, but the basins must be crossed in order
to reach it, and this is not an easy undertaking
even when their water supply is low, but in the
early summer they are almost full.

There are said to be more than one hundred
caves in Stone County, one of which is supposed
to be fully as large as Marble Cave, if not larger,

and is located in the southern part of the county but has not been explored.

Mill Cave is in the northeast of the county, and at the entrance is a saw mill which receives its working power from the cave stream. Inside the cave there is a lake.

Hermit's Cave is a few miles from Ga'ena, and is so named on account of having been used as a dwelling by its former owner, who kept a coffin in which he intended to place himself before the final summons, but was overtaken by death in the forest and it was never used. He wrote sermons on the rocks in his cave and one of these was afterwards removed.

Wolf's Den is also near Galena, and has been utilized as a sheep fold.

Wild Man's Cave is near Galena, and on account of the stories with which people have been frightened, can only be visited by permission and with a guard stationed at the entrance.

Reynard's Cave is four miles west of Galena on the farm of Dr. Fox, but is so nearly filled up with dripstone that only crawling room remains. The doctor's place is a fine locality for the collection of fossils.

At a distance of twelve miles from Galena there is said to be a fine natural bridge, well worth a visit and sufficiently near Mill Cave for both to be seen on the same trip.

In Bread Tray Mountain there is supposed to

be a cave through which a torrent rushes at
times, that being the only way in which to
explain the strange thundering, roaring noise
always heard after a storm, and never at other
times.

Besides being a wonderful cave region, and
rich in the great abundance and variety of native
fruits and fine timber, Stone County has a vast
amount of mineral wealth, the heaviest deposits
being zinc, lead and iron, with some indications
of silver, gold and copper, which have been
found but not in paying quantity. Already
since the summer of 1896 several exceptionally
pure bodies of zinc have been discovered, the
white ore of one recently opened deposit giving
highly gratifying indications as to extent.
Prospecting may be said to have only commenced
in this very far from over-crowded region.

CHAPTER VI.

OREGON COUNTY CAVES.

GREER SPRING.

Oregon County is also at the extreme southern limit of the State of Missouri and was visited, not because its caves are supposed to be either finer or more numerous than those of all the other Ozark counties, but on account of remarkable attractions associated with them that are not known to be equaled, or even subject to rivalry, by any similar works of nature in any portion of the world.

The most convenient railway point is Thayer; the station hotel affords comfortable accommodations for headquarters, and the last days of September proved a charming time. The foliage was in full summer glory, refreshed by a gentle and copious rain, and the insinuating tick had already retired from active business until the following season.

The carriage having been ordered on condition of its being a clear day, we left Thayer at eight o'clock on a perfect morning to visit Greer Spring, and were soon in the depth of the beautiful Ozark forest, from which we did not once

WILDERNESS PINERY, OREGON CO.

Page 84.

emerge until Alton, the county seat, was reached, the distance traveled being sixteen miles. Here we stopped for dinner at the small hotel kept by one of the old-time early settlers who came to the region before the war. The dinner was a surprise, and received the highest commendation possible to a dinner, the hearty appreciation of a boy. A young nephew, Arthur J. Owen, having been invited to act as escort on the trip, found all the varied experience in cave hunting fully equal to the pictured joys of anticipation. After a large bell suspended somewhere outside had notified the business public that dinner was ready to be served, we were invited to the dining-room, where on a long table was the abundance of vegetables afforded by the season and soil of an almost tropical state, and cooked as the white-capped chef of the great hotel, where the warm weeks were spent, had not learned the secret of; and the delicately fried chicken was not of that curious variety, commonly encountered by travelers, in which the development of legs robs the centiped of his only claim to distinction. As the dishes cooled they were removed and fresh supplies brought in.

Our driver received directions about the road and we started on another drive of seven miles. These directions were " to follow the main road to the forks, and then keep to the Van Buren road and any one could tell us where Captain Greer lives.''

The road was, as before. through the park-like forest, and as before, lay chiefly along the ridge, so that where clearings had been made for farms there were fine views over the distant country, which everywhere was forest-covered hills, of a rich green near at hand but changing with the growth of distance, first to dark, and then to lighter blue.

In these forests were fine young cattle and horses, and uncounted numbers of "razor-backs," or as they are otherwise called, "wind-splitters." For the benefit of those who may not be familiar with the names, it might be well to explain that they are the natural heirs of the native wild hog of Missouri and Arkansas. The nephew was greatly amused at seeing many of them with wooden yokes on their long necks, to prevent an easy entrance into fields and gardens by squeezing through the spaces between fence rails. These animals are such swift runners it is said they can safely cross the railroad between trucks of the fast express. Their snouts are so long and thin, it is also claimed that two can drink from a jug at the same time; never having seen it done, however, this is not vouched for, but merely repeated as hearsay.

After a time we stopped to inquire the way of an old man dipping water from a pond by the roadside. He told us he was dipping water to wash the wheat he was sowing in the field just over the fence, and that we reach the forks, then to keep the Van Buren road, pass two houses on the left, a white one on the right, another on the left and then inquire the way—anyone could tell us, and Captain Greer would show us to the Spring, "for he is a mighty accommodating man."

On we went to the forks where in the point of the Y stood a large tree with a Van Buren sign-board on one side, and in the direction it pointed, we turned, although rather reluctantly, for it looked little used and rocky, while the other was in good condition; but we followed the sign-board and had no misgivings until it began to be realized that a great deal of time was being passed but no houses. The morning had been very chilly, but now the atmosphere was just at that balmy point between warm and cool that makes mere living an unqualified luxury; and added to this we soon found ourselves in a deep cañon no less beautiful than the justly celebrated North Cheyenne Cañon near Colorado Springs.

There was now no doubt that we were on the wrong road, but such magnificence was unexpected and not to be turned from with indifference.

For some distance the road makes a gradual and rather perilous looking descent along the

steep and broken slope on the shady side of the
ancient river's great retaining-wall, while that
opposite is glorified by the brilliant glow of the
afternoon sun, which adds an equal charm to the
rich, luxuriant foliage below and the tall stately
pines that adorn, without concealing, the grey
rock they proudly cling to, or that rises in a
protecting rampart three hundred feet higher
than the cañon bed, with banners of the long-
needled pine waving above to proclaim the perfection of Nature's undisturbed freedom.

The road descending crosses the thread of
water still flowing among the great rounded
bowlders left by the former torrent, and our view
is changed to one of dense, but by no means
melancholy, shadows, with a crown of golden
sun-light; and presently the course of the cañon
turns to the east, and it is all filled with the
yellow rays and we notice the bright red haw-
thorn berries, and masses of hydrangea still
showing remnants of their late profusion of
bloom. We Missourians have a great love of
fine scenery and generally take long journeys
into other states in order to gratify the taste,
while quite unconscious of the wonderful beauty
and grandeur of the Ozarks.

Where the cañon begins to broaden into a
small sheltered valley as it approaches Eleven
Points River, we turned and retraced our way
to the forks, and a short distance beyond to a

house where we might again inquire. A woman came to the open door as we stopped and in answer to a question said: "You ought to have asked me when you passed here a while ago."

Apologies for the seeming neglect were offered and accepted, then she explained that both roads went to Van Buren but not to Greer Spring, where in due time we at length arrived.

The house being in one corner of a "forty" and the spring in that diagonally opposite, there was a walk of nearly that distance before coming to an old road inclining steeply down into what looked to be a narrow cañon. About midway of this sloping road, the space confined between perpendicular walls, rising to heights above on one side and descending to the stream on the other, widens suddenly and a picturesque old mill comes into view, it having been wholly screened from the approach by the rich growth of shrubs and trees. Chief in abundance among this luxury of leaf was the hydrangea,—a favorite shrub largely imported into this country from Japan before it was discovered as a native. The mill site seems to have been selected for its beauty although we were told that at this point the stream is seventy-two feet wide, and two and one half feet deep, but could be raised thirty feet with perfect safety by a dam, for which the rock is already on the ground and much of it broken

ready for use. The flow is said to be two hundred and eighty yards per minute, with no
appreciable variation, and never freezes. The
high walls of the Greer Spring gorge will, of
course, far more than double the value it would
otherwise possess, when it becomes desirable
to control and turn to practical account the
power now going so cheerily to waste, but the
artistic loss will be proportionately severe.

The old mill was the scene of great activity
in former times, but was closed on account
of an unfortunate accident and for years has
had no other duty than simply to serve as a
portion of the landscape.

Just beyond, the cañon makes a curving bend,
the road dwindles to a narrow path and we
behold the most beautiful scene imaginable.

The cañon has come to an end and is shut in
by a graceful curve of the high, perpendicular
grey walls that are crowned with trees and
shrubs, and decked below with a thick carpet of
bright green moss. In this basin, which is
nearly one hundred feet across, Greer Spring
plunges up from beneath through an opening
nine feet in diameter, in the midst of a pool of
water six feet deep, and having an unvarying
temperature of forty-nine degrees throughout
the year. This water is so perfectly clear that
not the least pebble is obscured from view, and
the color scheme is most marvelous.

GREEK SPRING.

Page 88.

Where the great spring forces its way to the surface, the water is a deep, brilliant blue with white caps, and its falling weight keeps clear of moss a large spot of fine, pure, white sandstone, while all the balance appears a vivid green from the moss that thrives beneath the moving water; and surrounding these are the handsome, foliage-decked grey walls. The edges of the basin are thickly strewn with fallen rocks deeply covered with moss, in which small ferns are growing, and on these gay stepping stones we crossed to the head-wall of the cañon to find ourselves at the open mouth of a cave from which flows a clear, shallow stream to join the waters of the Spring in that wonderful basin. The entrance to the cave is an arch about fifteen feet wide and twelve feet high, with the clear, shallow stream spreading over the clean rock floor from side to side. Here now was presented a difficulty. Truly the cave was *not* quite dry. The water was about ten inches deep, and my boots in Thayer. Contrary to advice, however, my nephew had brought his, and with a boy's kindness loaned them while he made the trip with bare feet and rolled up trousers.

A short distance within, the cave widens and the floor of the extension being somewhat higher, is dry, but the roof drops so low over it that the water-course is an easier route of travel; and this soon widens into a lake above which the cei'ing rises in a broad dome less than twenty feet in height, and hung with heavy masses of dripstone draperies of varying length, from five to seven feet; and all the ceilings are fringed at various heights with stalactites of every size and age, some being a clear, colorless onyx, while others proclaim their great age in the fact that they have so deteriorated that the onyx texture is either partly or completely lost, and what was once a pure drip crystal has returned to a common, porous, dull-colored limestone so soft that portions can be rubbed to powder in the hand.

Picking the way carefully as the depth of the lovely lake increased, we followed the sound of falling water and peered into the dark distance in a vain effort to see it, yet expecting to reach that special object of interest by keeping to the shallower parts of the lake. These expectations were shattered suddenly when the boots filled with water, and that called to mind the fact that twenty-three miles and a chilly night lay between us and dry clothing; so we returned to the outside world and rested on the rocks where Captain Greer and our young driver waited for us. The cave has never been fully explored, and probably we penetrated farther than others have ever done, as the owner knew nothing of the falling water we so distinctly heard and were surely very near.

The view from the rocks is wonderfully beautiful and includes both the entrance to the cave, with its flowing stream, and the receiving basin with its bounding stream. But it was growing late in the afternoon, and there was another cave whose entrance was in the perpendicular wall above the end of the path by which we had come. This entrance could be reached by a dilapidated ladder; assisted by a forked pole and supplied with candles and matches, my nephew and I achieved the ascent with not much trouble. Here we found what is, no doubt, one of the oldest caves known.

The original cavity is nearly filled up with masses of onyx—colorless crystal and white striped with pale shades of grey. The cave is perfectly dry and freshly broken surfaces in some places show signs of deterioration, so how can we venture even a guess as to the time it has required to first excavate the cave and then fill it with masses of rock deposited by the slow drip process, and later, for that crystalline rock in a now dry atmosphere to present a perceptible weakening? We went as far as passages could be crawled into, which was no great distance, and at once started on our uncertain descent of the ladder; but this was not a matter of so much concern as the upward trip, for the success of which some doubts were entertained; for going down is always naturally a less certain matter, as one can fall if more desirable means are unsuccessful, and I have unexpectedly reached many coveted points in this simple manner.

Taking a last look at Greer Spring with its cave river, grey walls, gay with foliage, and all the harmony of color and form combined in the narrow cañon that was once the main body of a great cave, I recalled views on the Hudson River and in the mountains of Maryland, Virginia and Pennsylvania, and others out in the Rocky Mountains in Colorado and the Wausatch in Utah, but amid all their wonderful grandeur and famous beauty, could remember no spot superior to this masterpiece of the Ozarks.

The proprietor of the Spring and a thousand acres of land adjacent, took personal possession on the day of Lincoln's first election, to establish a home.

The sun having failed to consider our wishes was now about to disappear in a gleaming flood of gold, so the return to Thayer that night was out of the question. Our host and his wife observed that fact and cordially invited us to remain for the night and as much longer as we would like to, but being unwilling to impose on kindness to such an extent, we returned to the hotel in Alton, and now urgently advise that those who ever have an opportunity to enjoy a moonlight drive through the Ozark forests should not let it pass unimproved.

OTHER CAVES NEAR BY.

About twelve miles from Alton there are three other caves worthy of attention. Two of these are known only as The Saltpetre Caves, and the third as The Bat Cave.

Not many persons care to visit the Bat Cave, for although its inhabitants are small, they have evidently decided to profit by the experience of the Red Man and take no risks through hospitality. Their warnings can be heard like distant thunder for some distance outside the cave, and any unheeding intruder is set upon in fury by such vast numbers of the little creatures that his only safety is in hasty retreat.

During the war the two Saltpetre Caves were worked to a considerable extent, and also served as safe retreats for the residents of the region, as well as the visiting "Jonny," when the vicinity became oppressively "blue."

Both of these caves are especially notable on account of the fine stalactites with which they are abundantly supplied; most of them being snow white and from fourteen to twenty feet in length.

Unfortunately, most of the caves in this region have been deprived of great quantities of their

beautiful adornments by visitors who are allowed
to choose the best and remove it in such quantities as may suit their convenience and pleasure.
Those who own the caves, and those who visit
them, would do well to remember that if all the
natural adornment should be allowed to remain
in its original position, it would continue to
afford pleasure to many persons for an indefinite
time; but if broken, removed, and scattered the
pleasure to a few will be comparatively little
and that short-lived. The gift of beauty should
always be honored and protected for the public
good.

We were not so fortunate as to discover fossils
of any kind in this locality, although the search
was by no means thorough; but even if it had
been the result might have been the same, since
that county and others adjoining have been
mapped as Cambrian. The greater part of the
exposed rock is a fine sandstone almost as white
as gypsum on a fresh fracture, and much of it
is ripple-marked so as to show a beautifully
fluted surface of remarkable regularity. These
ripple flutings are sometimes more than an inch
in width, and often less, but the variations never
appear on the same level, the smallest being seen
on the hill-tops and the larger outcropping on
the downward slopes.

CHAPTER VII.

THE GRAND GULF.

Oregon County, Missouri, is also fortunate in having within its limits the Grand Gulf, which has been declared by competent judges to be one of the wonders of the world; and it offers a combination of attractions that certainly entitles it to an important place among a limited few of America's choicest scenes.

The Gulf is nearly nine miles northwest of Thayer, Missouri, and about equally distant from Mammoth Spring in Arkansas, just a little south of the Missouri state line. The drive is a pleasant one, as the road winds among the forest-clad hills and passes occasional fields of cotton and corn; but having been macadamized in very ancient times by the original and all-powerful general government of that early period is somewhat rough, yet threatens no danger greater than the destruction of wheels.

The only approach to the Gulf is over the hill-tops; and the entrance in past times, while it was still a cave, must have been a sink-hole in the roof of the largest chamber. This chamber is now the upper end of the Grand Gulf, and into

it we descended by a rugged path, sufficiently
difficult to maintain expectations of grandeur
that are not doomed to disappointment. The
precipitous walls, two hundred feet in height,
bear a faithful record of the energy of circling
floods ; but instead of frowning, as some good
people persistently accuse all noble heights of
doing, they seem to look with conscious pride
towards the windings of the great rough chasm,
where every available spot has been seized on
as a homestead for some form of vegetation. All
the great, dark rock masses that interfere with
easy progress along the lowest depth, were surrounded by a feathery setting of blooming white
agaratum ; and each turn in the winding course
reveals new charms of rock and verdure with
their varying lights and shadows until the
crowning glory is reached at the Natural Bridge,
about twelve hundred feet from the upper end
of the canon. This bridge is magnificent. It
was impossible to secure photographs because
the abrupt curve by which it is approached
gave no point of view for a small camera ; and it
was equally impossible to reach desirable points
for taking measurements, but the open arch is
not less than twenty feet wide and considerably
more than that in height. From the floor or
bed of the Gulf to the road that crosses the
bridge is more than two hundred feet. The
passage under the bridge makes a curve, the

shortest side of which measures exactly two
hundred and nineteen feet, and as the width
varies from twenty to forty feet, the other side
is longer. Most of the floor is flat and level as
also is the ceiling, the greatest irregularities
being along the wall of greater length which
shows at what points the rushing water has spent
its force. No water flows through here now
except in times of heavy rainfall. The other end
of the bridge has a somewhat smaller span but is
very handsome, and the outward views from
both are exceedingly fine. After traversing
about four hundred feet more of the beautiful,
high-walled Gulf, we stood before the grand
entrance to the cave, which is strikingly similar
to the first arch of the bridge. The only picture
I was able to get was taken from the slope of the
Bridge-crown, one hundred feet below the road,
and merely gives a suggestion of the magnificence
waiting peacefully for the crowds of eager and
enthusiastic sight-seers who will in the near
future rush to this charming region in the ''Land
of the Big Red Apple.''

My companions were the same as mentioned
in the preceding chapter, a nephew, James
Arther Owen, and an obliging, tall young man
of twenty, who acted as guide and driver.

Relieving ourselves of all superfluous burdens
just within the cave entrance, we lighted candles
and sat down to wait for our eyes to adjust

themselves to the changed condition, from brilliant sunlight to absolute darkness, broken only by the feeble strength of three candles. It was noticeable that in the moist atmosphere of the Missouri caves, three candles were not more than equal to one in the dry caves of South Dakota.

Very soon we were able to continue the inspection of our surroundings, and the large passage we were in would more properly be called a long chamber, of irregular width but averaging about thirty feet. This ends abruptly nearly five hundred feet from the entrance, but a small passage scarcely more than six feet high runs off at right angles, and into this we turn. It is not quite so nearly dry as the outer chamber, and at a distance of less than one hundred feet we suddenly come to the end of dry land at an elbow of the silently flowing river whose channel we had almost stepped into. The ceiling dipped so we were not able to stand straight, and the guide said he had never gone farther; but to his surprise here was a light boat which I am ready to admit he displayed no eagerness to appropriate to his own use, and swimming about it, close to shore, were numerous small, eyeless fish, pure white and perfectly fearless; the first I had ever seen, and little beauties.

By burning magnesium ribbon we saw that the passage before us was a low arch and occupied from wall to wall by water, the direction of the flow being into another of somewhat greater size at right angles to that by which we had come, and at the mouth of this lay the boat. The distance we could see in either direction was of tantalizing shortness, and the boat was provided with no means of guidance or control, save an abundance of slender twine which secured it to a log of drift from the outside; so I decided to leave my companions in charge of the main coil of twine while I went on an excursion alone, there being not much evident cause for apprehension as no living cow could ever have made the trip to this favored spot.

Although the water looked perfectly placid, the boat drifted with surprising speed, so that the two scared faces peering after me were soon lost sight of. The channel was nowhere more than six feet wide, consequently as the boat inclined to drive against either wall I was able with care to keep it off the rocks with my hands, and in the same way guide it around the sharp turns in safety. After several of these turns there appeared the mouth of a passage so much smaller that the roof was only twelve inches above the sides of the boat and I could touch both walls at the same time. By running the boat across this it was held in place by the current, and I could sit at ease and enjoy the position, which even the least imaginative

person can readily conceive to have been a
novel one.

The small eyeless fish had been noticeable in
the water everywhere but now came swimming
about the boat in an astonishing multitude, and
as unconscious of any possible danger as bees in
a flower garden. Having no eyes, they were
naturally undisturbed by the light, so the candle
could be held close to the water for a satisfactory examination of the happy creatures.

They bore a striking resemblance to minnows,
although a few were larger, and it is claimed
that four or five inches are sizes not unusual,
but they happened not to be on exhibition.
Even dipping a hand into the water in their
midst occasioned no alarm, and they might
have been caught by dozens.

The guide now loudly called that he had fears
of the twine being cut on the sharp edges of
rock, and that cutting off all possibility of the
boats return, which being sufficiently reasonable, explorations were indefinitely suspended,
and a landing soon made. The camera and
flash-light were then prepared for taking a view,
and a point of light being needed to work by the
nephew was asked to sit in the boat with his
candle, to which he readily consented; but judg-
ing from the developed picture it may be
doubted if his pleasure at the time was extremely keen.

On leaving the cave the guide said it would
not be necessary to return to the upper end of
the Gulf in order to reach the surface, as the
ascent could be made in another place; and
leading the way to the left of the entrance he
started up the nearly perpendicular wall, more
than two hundred feet high, by a sort of "blind
trail" that would have caused a mountain
sheep to sigh for wings, but it was very beautiful.

We walked over to the wagon road on the
high ridge above the middle of the bridge and
going down the forest-clad slopes to the perpendicular wall in which is the smaller of the great
arches, admired from this fair point of view
the marvelous grandeur of one of the greatest
natural wonders.

The weather being perfect after a rain the
day before, there was no need of haste to get in-
doors, so we lingered into the afternoon and
then drove to the Mammoth Spring, in Arkansas,
a short distance south of the Missouri state line,
where the Cave River, just visited, comes to the
surface in a bounding spring of great force.
The distance being little less than nine miles.

The basin filled by the Spring might be called
a lake, as its size of two hundred by three hundred feet gives it that appearance, and the color
is a remarkable deep blue. The volume of
water is so nearly uniform that the height

seldom varies more than two or three inches, but three years ago a storm of unusual violence carried out most of the native fish, and in restocking from Government supplies, the clear, cold water suggested an experiment with mountain trout which are found to be doing well.

Where Mammoth Spring flows out its power is utilized by a flour mill on one bank and a cotton mill on the other, and the water flowing on forms Spring River, well known for the charm of its beautiful scenery.

This Spring is described by Dr. David Dale Owen in his First Report of a Geological Reconnoissance of the northern counties of Arkansas, 1857 and 1858, pp. 60-61.

CHAPTER VIII.

THE BLACK HILLS AND BAD LANDS.

In order to thoroughly appreciate and enjoy the wonderful caves of South Dakota, which are found within the limits of the Black Hills, it is necessary to have some knowledge of the geological character and history of that peculiar region.

Prof. J. E. Todd, State Geologist, in his "Preliminary Report on the Geology of South Dakota," gives an interesting "Historical Sketch of Explorations" in his state, beginning with the expedition of Captains Lewis and Clark to the upper Missouri regions in 1804 –6 to explore that portion of the recent Louisiana Purchase for the government and notify the Indians of the transfer; and including all other important expeditions since that time down to his own official tour of the Black Hills and Bad Lands in 1894. His own descriptions are so concise and graphic as to invite quotation. Of the Hills he says:

"The Black Hills have an area of five-thousand square miles of a rudely elliptical form with its major axis, approximately, north-northwest.

Most of this area lies within our state. The true limit of the Hills is quite distinctly marked by a sharp ridge of sandstone, three hundred to six hundred feet in relative height, which becomes broader and more plateau-like towards the north and south ends. This ridge is separated from the higher mass of hills within by a valley one to three miles in breadth, which is known as the Red Valley, from its brick-red soil, or the 'race course,' which name was given it by the Indians because of its open and smooth character, affording easy and rapid passage around the Hills. The junction of the outer base of the Hills with the surrounding table lands has an altitude of three thousand, five hundred to four thousand feet. Within this Red Valley one gradually ascends the outer slope of the Hills and soon enters, at an altitude of four thousand five hundred or five thousand feet, the woody portion of the region. This outer slope varies greatly in width and is underlaid by older sedimentary rocks, cut in almost every direction by narrow deep cañons. This feature covers nearly the whole of the western half of the Hills proper, where erosion has been less active on account of its distance from the main channels of drainage. Usually, from the broken interior edge of this slope or sedimentary plateau one descends a bluff or escarpment, and enters the central area of slates, granite, and quartzites, which is carved into high ridges and sharp peaks cut by many narrow and deep valleys and ravines and generally thickly timbered with the common pine of the Rocky Mountains. Toward the south, about Harney Peak, the surface is peculiarly rugged and difficult to traverse. Toward the north, also, about Terry and Custer peaks, a smaller rugged surface appears; but in the central area between and extending west of the Harney range is a region which is characterized by open and level parks much lower than the surrounding peaks and ridges.''

The Archæan rocks which form the core of the Hills mark the center of the various uplifts which have attended their formation and controlled their history. The coarse granite of Harney Peak indicating that, as the central point of the earli st upheaval, and the three porphyries known as rhyolite, trachyte, and phonolite, showing the uplifts of later periods to have had their centers a little more to the north, but the entire area is said to be only about sixty miles long and twenty five miles in width. It is exceptionally rough and mountainous, and consequently has great charms for the lover of fine scenery. Erosion has only partially denuded the peaks of the sedimentary rocks through which they were thrust up, or by which they were overlaid during the earlier part of

several subsequent periods of submersion.   The
Hills, in those remote times, led but a doubtful
and precarious existence, being now an isolated
island rising out of a shallow sea, and then,
owing to a general subsidence, submerged in
the ocean to so great a depth that even Harney
Peak is supposed to have almost, if not entirely,
disappeared. This up and down motion continued at intervals until the Fox Hills epoch of
the Cretaceous Age, at the close of which the
sea retired forever from that portion of the
country. In the next epoch fresh water work began and extensive marshes were formed, with an
abundant growth of vegetation and reptiles.
There was also much volcanic violence which
resulted in the fine scenery in the north end of
the Black Hills, and probably opened the fissures
to form Wind Cave, the Onyx Caves in the
southern hills and Crystal Cave near the eastern
edge toward the north. This was near the close
of the Cretaceous Age. But here is a point on
which the best authorities who have studied the
porphyry peaks, have failed to agree; Prof. N.
H. Winchell believing that the intrusion occurred, probably, during the Jura Trias, but as
Cretaceous beds, of more recent date, are found
to have been distorted by the outflow, it seems
that Professors Todd, Newton and Carpenter
hold the stronger position and that the later
time is correct.

No record of the next geological stage, which was the Eocene, or earlier part of the Tertiary Age, has been found in the Hills, because they were at that time dry land with gently flowing, shallow streams, and consequently no strata were laid down; but they are supposed, through later evidences, to have had a tropical climate and vegetation, enjoyed by large animals of strange new forms. The volume of fresh water afterwards became so great that immense lakes spread over large portions of the west, one of which occupied most of the region around the Black Hills at the beginning of the Miocene, and animal life was more abundant than ever before and of higher orders, many species being the same as are now in existence. The weather became more and more inclement and as the storms increased the erosion of the Hills also increased, and the rivers changed to torrents with deep channels. Earthquakes are supposed to have occurred and also volcanic eruptions.

The Black Hills were now rising steadily, and as the slope of the streams increased, the channels cut deeper, and the fissures now known as caves had long been filled with water.

The most important of the numerous animals of the Tertiary Age yet discovered in the Hills and surrounding region, are the Titanotherium or Brontotherium, similar to our Hippopotamus, the Oreodon, and a small horse having three

toes on each foot.   A little later in the same Age
the horses were similar to those of the present
time and of equal size, which proves that the
wild horses of the West were not descended from
the few lost by the Spanish Invaders.   At this
time the first lions, camels, mastodons, and
mammoths also appeared.   The remains of these
animals are so abundant in places as to indicate
that they perished in herds that were overwhelmed suddenly by great floods, and many,
no doubt, huddled together and perished with
cold; for with the beginning of the present age
the Hills had reached their highest elevation,
the inclement weather increased, and the tropical climate suddenly changed to one extremely
cold.   It was the beginning of the Glacial
Period or Ice Age, when a large portion of the
United States is supposed to have been covered
by a sheet of ice.   The ice is believed to have
entered South Dakota from the northeast and its
drift across the state limited by a line so closely
following the present course of the Missouri
River that many of us would be inclined to consider it the western bluff.   Beyond this line the
ice failed to push its way, but the Hills were
subject to heavy rain storms that filled the
streams and carried large quantities of bowlders
and other eroded material, both coarse and fine,
down into the valleys and over the lower hills,
where much of the moderately coarse can now

be seen exposed on the surface, and fine specimens collected without the use of a hammer.
The brilliantly colored, striped and mottled
agates, and the bright, delicate tints of the
quartz crystal, are particularly attractive to the
majority of visitors. The beauty of these gaily
colored rocks is quite extensively utilized by the
inhabitants of the southern and southeastern
hills to supply the place of growing plants which
are generally denied by the inconvenience of the
water supply. The quartzite of the Hills is well
crystallized and heavy. I have one beautiful
specimen of the dark Indian red variety through
which passes a narrow line of pale blue, and the
yellow quartzite or jasper sometimes shows
dendrite markings. Very great quantities of
agates and jasper, mostly in small pieces, but
unlimited variety, are to be seen in portions of
the Bad Lands, south of the fork of the Cheyenne
River, with an almost equal abundance of
baculites and numerous other fossils.

The wide expanse of deep ravines and sharp,
barren ridges in the Bad Lands is a unique
departure from the usual phases of natural
scenery that inspire interest and wonder, but no
great admiration, until one soon learns that the
law of compensation has been strictly observed.
The beauty of vegetation denied those desolate
buttes and ridges is atoned for by a marvelous
abundance of most wonderful crystals of aragon-

ite, calcite, barite and satin spar; each to itself,
or two or more combined in beautiful geodes or
else arranged in great flat slabs crystallized on
both sides of a thin sheet of lime. These slabs
are composed of crystals of uniform size and of
a pale green tint. But the geodes show some
striking combinations of both crystals and colors
with an exterior formed like box work, composed of a very heavy dark material said to
be a mixture of barium, calcium and iron. The
interior may be a bright green or lemon yellow, or
perhaps the two in combination, while others
yet may be either of these varieties with the
addition of flat crystals of almost transparent
satin spar. These crystals also occur in masses
of the same box-like formation rising just
so much above the surface of the barren ridge
they occupy as to give it the appearance of a
prairie dog town. One hill-top over which an
abundance of detached crystals, of the palest
water-green tint, has been spread, gave the impression of being covered with crushed ice.
This transformation from a richly tropical to a
marvelously barren region, was accomplished
during the time when storms reigned over the
Hills and ice ruled the country to the north and
east.

The long slender barite crystals of a bright
golden brown color are especially beautiful but
are generally seen in the specimen stores, as the

deposit is confined to limited areas and the few persons familiar with the locations are not over anxious to introduce the general public.

The fossil remains previously referred to are of course only a few of the most important, but it is remarked as a curious and notable fact that among the fossils of the lower orders of life in the Bad Lands, the heads have not been preserved. On account of scarcity of water it is necessary for parties to carry a supply even when they expect to be in the vicinity of the Cheyenne River and probably ford the South fork, as these waters carry in solution a quantity of alkali that renders them unfit for drinking, although the effects would not be fatal but simply the extreme reverse of pleasant.

No caves have been discovered in the Bad Lands, unless that name be applied to some of the geodes which are really grottoes, they being of sufficient size for a man to stand in. The Black Hills, however, contain some of the most remarkable caves ever yet discovered, of which those of greates timportance are Wind Cave and the three Onyx Caves near Hot Springs, in the southeastern part of the Hills, and Crystal Cave near Piedmont, in the northeast. All of these occur in the Carboniferous Limestone which forms an outer belt around the central mass or core of the Hills and no doubt, as previously suggested, owes its fissures to earthquakes which preceded or accompanied the porphyry intrusions by which in some localities its strata have been thrown into a vertical position.

CHAPTER IX.

WIND CAVE.

Wind Cave was discovered in 1881 by a hunter named Thomas Bingham, who being weary of a fruitless chase sat down to rest, and was soon startled by the sound of rushing wind on a calm day; and at the same time by a singular hair-raising sensation, as his hat was lifted from his head and thrown high in the air. He is said to have afterwards declared that although frightened nearly out of his wits, he determined to find the cause of his alarm, and on turning slightly discovered a hole about eight by twelve inches in size through which a roaring wind was issuing from the earth. As his hair maintained the aggressive attitude taken, the recovered hat could not be returned to its usual place, so an hour was spent in laying it across the opening and watching its instant projection into upper space; after which he set out to tell of the wonderful discovery. The announcement, however, was not received seriously and he was assured of the impossibility of the wind blowing through a hill of solid rock, and his brother explained to him that he had been too self-indul-

gent and consequently imagined the whole affair.
A protest of total abstinence failed to inspire
confidence, but the brother promised to go the
next day to see for himself, and did. The hat
was again placed over the opening as before, but
instead of taking the expected lofty flight, it
was drawn in and has never since been seen :
the current had reversed. Soon after this the
hole was enlarged to eighteen by thirty inches
and the cave entered by quite a number of ven-
turesome persons assisted by a long rope and
ample personal courage. No other improvements were made, and only a short distance
was explored, until Mr. J. D. McDonald settled
on the property in 1890; since which time he
and his sons have explored ninety-seven miles of
passage and done such extensive work in opening up small passages and placing ladders, that
it is now possible for visitors to travel long distances with surprising ease and comfort. The
measure of distances in the cave is not by the
usual guess-work method which has established
the short-measure reputation for cave miles, but
is done with a fair degree of accuracy by means
of the twine used to mark the trail in exploring
new passages. A careful measurement of the
twine has shown it to run nine balls to the
mile with a close average of regularity, so it is the
custom to add another mile to the cave record as
often as a ninth ball becomes exhausted.

Wind Cave is twelve miles north of Hot Springs by a good road which offers somewhat meager attractions to the artist, but is more liberal towards the geologist, and especially so in fine exposures of the gypsum bearing Red Beds of the Triassic. Limited patches of it are also exposed in each of the caves, generally carrying small quantities of selenite, which is crystallized gypsum, or in other words, crystallized sulphate of lime. This brilliant red color is so prominent in portions of the Hills, and attracts so much wondering attention in other well known regions of the West, that it would seem an unpardonable neglect of opportunity should we fail to again quote Prof. Todd for an explanation of the cause of the vivid coloring. Commencing he says: "Newton remarks concerning this: * 'A large percentage of peroxide of iron in the red beds, to which they owe their bright red color, bears an interesting relation to the absence of fossils. The material of which sediments are formed is derived, by the various processes of denudation, from the rocks of older land surfaces. Whatever iron they contain is dissolved from the land and transported in a condition of protoxide and some proto salt, such as the carbonate, and the process is facilitated by the presence of carbonic acid

* U. S. Geological Survey. Geology of the Black Hills. Henry Newton, p. 138.

in the water.   Now iron occurs in these
older rocks as protoxide and peroxide, the
former of which is soluble and the latter
insoluble in water.   The peroxide, however, by the action of organic matter, such as
is held in solution in boggy waters, may be
deprived of a portion of its oxygen and converted into protoxide and thus be rendered soluble.   If the iron-bearing water is confined first
in a shallow basin and exposed long to the action of the atmosphere the protoxide of iron
absorbs the oxygen and is precipitated as
an insoluble red peroxide of iron.   If,
however, plant or animal life be present in
sufficient quantities, this oxidation is prevented.
In case but little foreign material, clay or sand,
has been brought by the waters, the deposit
will be an iron ore.   In case large quantities of
foreign material are deposited from the waters
at the same time, there will be produced, in the
absence of life, a brown or red clay or sandstone,
and in its presence a white or light colored formation containing the iron as a carbonate.   We
reason therefore from the condition in which
the iron is found in the red beds, that there
could have been little or no life, animal or vegetable, in the water from which it was deposited.   The conclusion is strengthened by the
fact of the large quantities of gypsum which
are usually derived from the evaporation of saline

waters. The degree of saline concentration which the precipitation of gypsum indicates, would be highly inimical to life. The presence of gypsum helps to account for the absence of life, and the absence of life accounts for the brilliant color. The three prominent characteristics of the formation (that is the red beds) are therefore quite in harmony with each other.' " (Geol. Blk. Hills, p. 138.)

Continuing the subject, Professor Todd says: " Accepting this explanation of the striking red color, the question remains as to how these circumstances, favorable for its formation, were produced.

" This red color is quite common in the whole Rocky Mountain region, not only on the eastern slope of the mountains, but to the various detached members of the system. We must, therefore, look for some extensive condition. If we seek some case in the present, parallel to the one already indicated, we perhaps can find none better than one on the eastern shore of the Caspian Sea, where, because of dry climate and the shallow waters, the deposition of gypsum and salt is now going on. In the gulf known as the Kara Boghaz, which is separated from the Caspian by a narrow strait, the evaporation is so rapid as to produce an almost constant flow from the sea into it. This strait and this gulf give the impression to an unlearned observer that there must be a mysterious subterranean outlet. The water flows in, carrying with it the salt and other soluble minerals. It then evaporates, leaving the salt and minerals behind.''

This explanation is calculated to afford particular pleasure to the many visitors to the Garden of the Gods, in Colorado, who seldom receive satisfactory answers to their questions as to the reasons '' why.'' In that much visited spot, however, the great mass of the deposit has been removed by erosion and the curiously shaped remnants are only such portions as were exceptionally hard and consequently withstood the action of the submerging waters.

Having made a considerable stop on the way to Wind Cave, we will now hurry on, but with good horses and a fine day the drive is one of great pleasure. The road gradually rises to higher ground and soon reaches a point six hundred feet more elevated than Hot Springs, with a charming view of hill and valley distances, and the way then continues over the hill-tops. At one point by the roadside a circle of tent-stones still marks the spot occupied by Sitting Bull for a week or more after the Custer massacre, while he camped here and in the security of his commanding position watched the movements of the government troops who were in search of him.

Hot Springs and Buffalo Gap are both included in the wide-spread view. Beside the road and scattered about in all directions are fine speci mens of agates and quartz crystal which seem most beautiful and most abundant on the hills in the immediate vicinity of the cave, the crys- tals being either rose pink, pale green, yellow, white or colorless.

Arriving at the cave, the entrance is not vis- ible, but between the ravine in which it is located and the road, there is the cave office and small hotel, on the ravine side of which an outer stairway leads down to the cave entrance, over which has been built a log cabin.

On account of the precautions taken for the protection of visitors, accidents are so rare that it might almost be said that none occur. Every person is required to register before entering the cave and all returning parties are carefully counted, although they are usually unaware of the fact. They are always accompanied by two guides and others are added if the party is large. No one is, on any account, permitted to wander in advance of the head guide or linger behind the one in the rear.

Within the cabin the immediate entrance to the cave is securely closed, and in order that the door may not be forced from its fastenings by the roaring wind which shakes it threaten- ingly, it opens in, instead of out. This wind

suggested the name Wind Cave, and will probably be utilized, at no very distant time, to gen-
erate electricity for lighting the cavern.

The wind is strongest at the surface, and a
guide goes down first to place lights in
sheltered nooks where the force has begun to
diminish, about fifty feet below the entrance;
and here we light our candles which, if guarded
somewhat, are not extinguished unless the current is unusually severe. The balance of the
descent of one hundred and fifty-five feet from
the surface to the first chamber is easily accomplished.

This would be the least interesting room in
the cave if it were not the Bride's Chamber, on
account of having once been the scene of a mar-
riage ceremony. But no others are in need of
assistance of such romantic nature, as all are
curiously and handsomely decorated, with such
a charming variety of deposits, artistically
massed, combined or contrasted, that every step
brings fresh pleasure, and monotony is nowhere.

Passing from this room by a long, narrow
passage, in the walls of which are observed
many beautiful little pockets of crystals,
attention is presently called to Lincoln's Fire-
place, a perfectly natural specimen of the old-
fashioned design broadly open in the chimney;
doubtless just such an one as Mr. Lincoln's good
mother hung the crane in and set the Dutch oven

before. A little beyond and on the opposite
side of the crevice is Prairie-dog town, not a
very extensive town, to be sure, but so true a
copy that one unfamiliar with the small animal
and his style of architecture would afterwards
easily recognize both. At one time his dogship
was carried away by a too eager collector, but a
letter to the suspected visitor brought him home
by the next freight.

The Dutch Clock occupies a position on a
shelf near by, and all southern visitors greet the
Alligator as a familiar friend, as all of us joy-
fully meet any acquaintance from home.

A long narrow passage, formerly a "tight
crawl," but later opened up by heavy blasting,
must be traversed before we come to the Snow
Ball Room, beautiful with round spots of
untinted carbonate of lime, as if fresh soft snow
had been thrown by the handful over walls and
ceilings, with the additional ornamentation of
calcite crystals. In the crevice beyond rises the
Church Steeple, diminishing regularly, though
roughly, in size, to a height of sixty feet, but
not degraded with the little squirming stairway
usually seen in Church spires.

The next room is the Post Office, in which we
are for the first time introduced to the greatest
peculiarity and most abundant formation known
to the cave. Being a newly discovered addition
to geology it has no scientific name and there-

fore is simply called box work, because it
resembles boxes of many shapes and sizes. The
formation of the box work is generally regarded
as an unexplained and unexplainable mystery,
but a careful study of various portions of the
cave shows it in all stages of development and
suggests a reasonable theory as to the cause of
its origin and variety of development. The
volcanic disturbances which have already been
discussed as having been responsible for the
various uplifts and depressions of the Black
Hills region, and also for opening the fissures
which gave the cave a beginning, must have
supplied the conditions that were necessary to
the formation of box work. And these preliminary conditions were merely cracks in the rock.
By the violence of earth movement the limestone
has been crushed, probably when the land was
undergoing depression, prior to the upheaval
which opened the great parallel fissures. The
varying hardness of the rock, as well as proxi-
mity to the surface, would readily account for
the difference in size of the fractures, which is
from one-half inch to twelve inches; the largest
being the most distant from the surface. That
this crushing was done before the salt waters
retired from the region, which was towards the
close of the Cretaceous Age, is sufficiently evident
in the fact that portions of the Red Beds show
similar fractures with the cracks filled with

gypsum, and gypsum, as we have already seen, is a salt water deposit.

After the crushing was done the cracks in the Carboniferous Limestone were filled with water heavily charged with calcium carbonate, taken in solution from the rock, first from pulverized particles, and afterwards by percolation and contact with exposed surfaces. This calcium carbonate was slowly deposited in crystalline form, so that in time the cracks were filled and the crushed rock firmly cemented with calcite seams. But in the meantime the removal of the calcium carbonate had started disintegration of the more exposed portions of the rock, which steadily continuing, finally reduced the porous body between the crystal seams to a soft clay which was gradually dissolved and carried out through small imperfections in the thin crystal sheets, leaving the empty box work as we find it. But where blasting has exposed fresh surfaces, much of the solid limestone carries the box-like sheets of crystal.

The thinnest box work is seen in the upper levels, from which the waters retired soonest, and the heaviest and most beautiful is in the Blue Grotto, on the eighth level where the water remained longest and its diminished volume became most heavily charged. In many places, however, there is another heavy variety known as pop-corn box work, which seems to be an

impure lime carbonate not so finely crystallized
as the other, but at the time of my visit no
explanation had been given of the manner of its
deposit; and my own theory that it was not
formed under water had nothing to sustain it
until, a few weeks later, while visiting Crystal
Cave, the work was found in active progress on
surfaces occupying every position, and the agent
was dripping water. In all cases the original
box work has been in thin sheets of calcite, and
the heavy varieties are due to later deposits
of calcite and aragonite crystals or, pop corn.

The colors are white, yellow, blue and choco-
late brown; the last named predominating to a
great extent in that portion of the cave most easily traveled by visitors, and forming the ceiling
and a part of one wall in the Post Office, where,
as has been said before, it first appears. The
effect is not dreary as might be imagined, and
parties are generally photographed here because
one side of the room is white and greatly assists
the flash. This is a smooth, perpendicular wall
marking the line of the fissure and showing the
strata of the rock in horizontal position whit-
ened with a thin coating of carbonate of lime.
All visitors are cordially invited to please themselves in leaving cards, letters or papers in this
chamber, which is reserved for that purpose,
and to refrain from leaving them in other por-

tions of the cave or defacing the walls with names.

Roe's Misery is a long, narrow passage into which, during the early times before its size had been increased by blasting, a large man named Roe crawled to his sorrow. Being larger than the hole he stuck fast, and neither his own efforts nor those of the guides could relieve the situation until a rope was sent for, and having been brought, was securely fastened to his feet, when a long pull and a strong one finally opened the passage. It is told that he claimed to have reviewed all the objectionable acts of his life, by which his friends understood that he occupied the motionless position not less than three weeks.

Red Hall is very nearly described by its name and is quite a showy room, with the bright red walls contrasting sharply with their limited ornamentation of pure white carbonate of lime and pearly crystals of calcite.

Off to one side of Red Hall is a beautiful little chamber called Old Maids' Grotto, probably on account of its trim appearance and ideal location. It is so entirely concealed from the view of those passing on the public highway, that its existence is not even suspected, until special attention is called to its cosiness, and then it is necessary to mount an accumulation of great water-rounded rocks in order to obtain convincing evidence of its actual reality. It is a long, narrow room, shut in by a straight wall sufficiently high for rigid seclusion, or protection, without preventing a glimpse of passing events.

A break in the description is made here for the purpose of inserting a description, written at the author's request, by Mr. E. L. McDonald. He was generally our special guide. He has chosen to describe the route taken by the majority of visitors and therefore the balance of my observations within those limits are omitted.

All who are familiar with those passages and chambers will observe while reading the next chapter that no imaginary attractions are added to the existing facts, but many interesting minor points are missing.

Only such changes are made as were agreed to as the condition on which he would attempt a piece of work so at variance with his usual occupations.

CHAPTER X.

THE FAIR GROUNDS ROUTE.

" At 9:30 in the morning the train bringing health-seekers and tourists arrives at Hot Springs, a beautiful little city nestled in the southernmost foot-hills of the world-reputed Black Hills of South Dakota. The choice of a hotel is soon made, and when located, the new-comers observe the other guests and acquaint themselves with the attractions of the resort. Probably during the day they are approached by the solicitor of the wonderful Wind Cave, who explains that the best way to reach the cave is by means of the coach and four seen at the hotel in the morning, and arrangements are made for the following day. The next morning, seated in the tally-ho coach with strangers who are soon acquaintances, you start on a beautiful twelve-mile drive to one of nature's most interesting sights.

"Immediately after leaving town you begin to admire the scenery and enjoy the cool, refreshing breezes, wafted from the mountains to the north, down the slopes to the arid plains.

127

" After climbing a gently sloping 'hog-back' for about eight miles, you are at the top of the divide and one thousand feet higher than Hot Springs, which may be seen on the left. Looking ahead you can see Harney Peak, the highest mountain in the Black Hills district; and on the right you see Buffalo Gap, through which the creek runs that heads at Min-ne-pa-juta Springs. The Indians used to drive buffalo through this gap, hence its name. A small but thriving little town to the eastward takes its name from this Buffalo Gap. From here you begin to go down a gentle and winding incline to the cave, which is reached all too soon.

"At the office you register and procure tickets, and then have from one-half to three-quarters of an hour in which to eat lunch or dine at the hotel. Then all congregate in the office, from whence the start is made, after every one has put on a cave cap, *not a suit, as such is entirely unnecessary*. The guide leads the way to the entrance of the cave which is separated from the office by some little distance, and is located in the bed of a long since dry run, which in former times has bared the carboniferous strata, and within this kind of rock the cave is found.

"As the author has asked me for an article descriptive of the cave, I will only attempt to say something of our medium length route to the Fair Grounds, or in other words, the Fair

Grounds' Route. A collective description of the whole cave would take months—even years—to complete. Besides, the above route is the one most used by visitors at the present time.

"On entering the Cave House (a log structure) you will in all probability ask from whence comes the murmur of a waterfall. The guide answers that it is the rushing current of air at the mouth of the cave, sometimes in and sometimes out. Prof. J. E. Todd, in bulletin No. 1, S. Dakota Geological Survey, p. 48, says: ' This phenomenon is found to correspond with the varying pressure of the barometer, and with its single opening and capacious chambers is easily accounted for.'

"The rushing air is sometimes strong enough to require a man's weight to open the entrance door. Five days and nights is the longest time the wind has been known to move in one direction without ceasing. This is one of nature's greatest atmospherical phenomena.

"Some one says, 'Tickets, please!' and into the hole we go, single file down a lighted passageway to where we can light our candles. After descending about one hundred and fifty-five feet we come into the Bridal Chamber (named by some of the earlier explorers before the present management took hold of the property), which is eight or ten feet in length by twenty feet in breadth. Passing along some distance, the

Snow-ball Room is entered. It carries this name on account of little rosettes of carbonate of lime sticking to the irregular ceiling. This room is pretty narrow and some fifty feet in length.

"The Post Office is next and soon reached. The ceiling is covered with the box work formation somewhat resembling Post Office boxes. You will no doubt wonder why it carries such a common name.

"Just because after searching in what books on geology and other sciences we could get, we could not find it described nor any formation resembling it; hence its common name, as we have named the pop-corn work, frost work etc., from their appearance.

"The dimensions of the Post Office are some eighty feet in length by twenty feet in width, with an average ceiling height of probably twelve feet. Red Hall is the room next in order, and has on either side a red bank of sandy, micaceous clay.

"Just to the left is a very pretty little grotto of box work. This room is very odd in make-up. The floor is very rough and dips about fifteen feet in its length of sixty feet, and includes a short flight of stairs. The lowest end of the room is prettily decorated, and some pleasing blends of color attract the eye. To the left is the Old Maids' Grotto, a pretty little nook that would please any maid old or young.

"After passing through the White Room we turn to the left along the crevice, and after traveling some little distance reach The Grand Opera, a very narrow room but some forty feet in length. Chopin's Nocturne is a small grotto in the right hand wall named by the famous violinist, Edouard Remenji.

"The Devil's Lookout is reached by a few steps. It is a crevice about ten feet wide at the base and sixty-five feet in height. This place is remarkable for its columns of rock just over head. The pathway leads to Milton's Study, some fifty feet distant. Turning into the crevice again, some twenty feet are traveled when attention is called to Seal Rocks. Sampson's Palace is the next room in order: here we see some stalagmitic water formation on the left wall and the ceiling is one of the most beautiful yet seen on the trip.

"We pass along to Swiss Scenery, a very prettily decorated room fifty feet in length by fifteen in height. The box work is very pretty, shading from yellow to dark brown. The general appearance of the room would suggest its name, it being rougher than any other in the immediate vicinity. Passing under an arch we enter the Queen's Drawing-room. Here the box work has been developed beyond any on our pathway thus far. From the ceiling it hangs like draperies and on the left wall is about twenty-four inches

in depth. On the whole this room is elegant
enough for the most exacting queen. We step
from this room into the M. E. Church. Rev.
Mr. Hancher, President of the Black Hills
Methodist College, was I believe the first to
hold song and prayer service in this room; the
pulpit is on the left as you pass through. The
guides always ask if any wish to sing or worship,
as any one has a perfect right in a dedicated
Chapel.

"The Giant's Causeway is only a few steps
beyond. This bit of scenery has some resemblance to the famed basalt attraction on the coast
of Ireland. We 'duck' our heads under the
Arch of Politeness and rise to a standing position
in Lena's Arbor, a very irregular shaped room
admired by a great many of our visitors.

"We enter Capitol Hall at the side, about
midway between the ends. It is the largest
room yet visited, being some two hundred feet
from end to end, with a very high ceiling. Here
we notice the walls and ceiling are bare of box
work and other formation, and are clean and
white. The decorative appearance exceeds any
room yet visited. After getting into line again
we go down a flight of stairs to Odd Fellows'
Hall, a chamber that on examination suggests its
name. In the ceiling is situated the 'All seeing
eye,' one of the emblems of that august body,
and at a little distance the 'Three links;' also

in the ceiling, and just under the latter is situated a rock very much resembling a goat.
Attention is called to the first appearance of
pop-corn work, a very peculiar formation resembling pop-corn after it has broken open, and in
this part of the cave it is quite plentiful.

"We now descend another flight of stairs into
Turtle Pass, where a large turtle rests beside
the path, and just beyond is the Confederate
Cross-roads, where the fissure is crossed by
another forming a cross with perfect right angles.
The right hand passage is used for specimens
only; straight ahead leads to the Garden of Eden,
the end of our shortest route; we take the left
hand path and journey through Summer Avenue,
some seventy feet in length, and reach the Scenes
of Wiclow, a large and high room, beautifully
decorated with box work and pop-corn. The
ceiling and the left wall from floor to ceiling are
fine box work. On the right you see dark space,
as a very large portion of this room is unused,
but we pass the Piper's Pig. List! The guide
is pounding on the Salvation Army Drum, a
large projecting rock that on being struck with
the closed hand gives a sound very much like a
bass drum.

"After walking across a short plank we enter
Kimball's Music Hall, a very beautiful room
settled between two crevices and lined with box
work. Viewing the ceiling from the fissure on

the right it is seen to be smooth and fringed
with pop-corn. In some places the boxes are
closed, resembling finished honey-comb. Over
head box work can be seen as high as the light
penetrates. On the whole, I think this is the
finest crevice in the explored cave.

"Looking straight ahead you wonder how the
party can travel over such a road as presents
itself to view, but the guide turns into an arch in
the right hand wall and enters Whitney Avenue.
After walking across the bridge over shadowy
depths, our pathway lies for some fifty feet in
one of the most interesting ovens in the cave,
at the end of which we enter Monte Cristo's
Palace by going down a flight of stairs. This
room has the greatest depth beneath the surface
of any of the Fair Grounds' Route, which is four
hundred and fifty feet. In this room is noticed
a decided change in the box work, which is
much heavier than any seen, or that will be
scene on this route, and the color is light blue.

"I guess I will give the party a talk while we
rest under Monte Cristo's Diamonds, a very
sparkling cluster, about six inches in diameter,
of silica crystals.

"After studying the cave, it appears that it
did not form in the same manner as most others;
on account of the absence of sink holes, the
regular arrangement of the chambers, the regular dip of the rock to the south-east from five to

ten degrees, and the regularity of the long vertical fissures running north-west south-east. In
fact, the whole cave is made up of these fissures
and it seems that the water has entered narrow
crevices opened by some eruptive force.

"You see small holes eaten in the ceilings and
walls in every direction, which indicates that the
water came from a higher level, and being under
great pressure, wanted passage out. It seems the
cave was a reservoir for a long time, then after the
water stopped flowing in it slowly receded, and
in settling the overcharged waters covered the
rocks and specimens with a calcareous coating,
very thin in the upper portions of the cave and
getting thicker the deeper you go, giving evidence as you see, of slowly settling. Had the
waters rushed out they would in all probability
have left the rocks uncoated as in all other
caves, with one exception, the Crystal Cave,
some seventy-five miles to the north of Wind
Cave.

"As we have some more caves to see we must
journey on.

"Taking one last look at Monte Cristo's Diamonds we pass into Milliner's Avenue, a very
pretty avenue indeed with nearly as many colors
as a milliner's show-window would present.
About mid-way of this avenue we cross the
bridge over Castle Garden, a room in the eighth
tier beneath the surface. From this avenue we

step into the Assembly Room. Here the
formations are covered with a gypsum crystal that sparkles with wonderful brilliancy.
On the right is a passage leading to the Masonic
Temple, a room that any body of Masons would
be proud of could they hold lodge meetings in it.
The passage on the left is the terminus of the
Pearly Gates' Route, the longest developed route
in the cave. After moving along some distance
we see the Bad Lands, and then come into the
Tennis Court. This room has the net in the
ceiling and I suppose the party can furnish the
raquet (racket). On the right hand side of this
room there is tier upon tier of box work; looking
to the left, you shudder at the almost bottomless
pit just beside the pathway. Here we take a rest
preparatory to climbing up to the Marble Quarry,
a task of two flights of stairs. This is a very
large room and has the most uneven floor, ceiling
and walls of any that our visitors see, and is
barren of specimens excepting in the first part
over the stairs where there is some box work of
very pretty structure and color. Some distance
up the path we see on one side the Ghost of
'She,' and on the other the Devil's Punch
Bowl, a large rock with a basin-shaped hole
about thirty-six inches across and sixteen inches
deep, but lo! the bottom has been broken out:
which is very appropriate as South Dakota is at
present a prohibition state. A winding path is

followed until attention is called to the Sheep's
Head above an arch over the passage, and the
ceiling here is of flint, the ledge of which is
four inches thick.

"Passing under the arch we enter Johnstone's
Camp Ground, so named because Paul Alexan-
der Johnstone camped in this room while accom-
plishing the third of his greatest mind-reading
feats, during which he remained in the cave
seventy-two hours. He was locked in his room
at the Evans Hotel while a committee secreted
the head of a gold pin in the cave. On their
return, after being blindfolded, he led them to
the livery stable, and securing a team drove to
the cave and found the pin in the Standing
Rock Chamber, beyond the Pearly Gates, and
then drove back to the city still blindfolded.

"Down one short flight of stairs and we are in
the Waiting Room, so called on account of persons waiting here while the rest of their party
finished the trip by climbing up the Alpine Way.
This difficult climb was made until the route was
developed via the Marble Quarry. A steep
pathway and one flight of stairs now bring us to
the Ticket Office, and another short stairway
leads into the room above, which is the Fair
Grounds. We enter the right wing, which
measures two hundred and six links in length
and forty-nine in width at the narrowest place.
We are now in the third level and no box work

is seen, but the ceiling (which is low) shows
many interesting fossils. The central dome is
some fifty feet in height, and passing to the
right the guide seats the party in such a position
that the frost work on the wall can be seen to
advantage. This is the largest part of the Fair
Grounds and measures six hundred and forty-
five links long, exclusive of the right wing, and
has a width of fifty-three links, which with
a number of wings added, makes it one of the
largest under-ground rooms within American
caverns.

"A great many visitors look at their cuff-buttons
when told we have twenty-five hundred rooms
included in ninety-seven miles of passageways.
Of course they do not understand how we get
the mileage. In going to the Fair Grounds we
travel about three miles. In each fissure there
are eight levels, which makes twenty-four miles
of cave from the entrance to the Fair Grounds.

"Of the formations in the cave, the different kinds are on different levels, the stalactites and stalagmites nearest the surface on
the second, the frost work on the third. This
formation is in most instances as colorless
as snow. The mode of its formation is not
thoroughly understood, but is found in such positions as suggest its being formed by vapors
overcharged as spoken of about the water. It is
almost always on an over-hanging rock, over or

near some fissure leading to a deeper portion of the cave. Box work in this level is scattering and fragile: in the fourth it is the prevailing formation: in the fifth it is heavier and a little darker; in the sixth it varies in style and color, and pop-corn appears, a queer formation resembling pop-corn ready to eat. It is not so purely white here as in the lower levels, seventh and eighth. In the seventh the box work is heavier than any seen on the Fair Grounds' Route and the color is nearly blue, having a faded appearance. In this tier is also found a good deal of mineral wool, which must not be mistaken for asbestos. It sometimes attains a length of eighteen inches and at one place where it seems to come out of a hole two inches in diameter, and drops down like a grey beard, we have named it Noah's Beard.

"In the eighth tier we find very beautiful formations of carbonate of lime, and the box work is decidedly blue, the boxes larger, and their partitions one half inch thick.

"We have been deeper than the eighth tier but in narrow crevices barely admitting a man of average stature. In these the calcareous coating is much thicker than in any higher portions of the cave, but very little sign of box work is seen.

"Sometimes we make a comparison between the cave and a sponge. Take for instance a sponge as large as an apple barrel and there would be holes in it as big as a man's thumb and closed hand. Now take a sponge, four miles square and five hundred feet deep with holes in proportion to the little sponge, and you have an illustration of The Wonderful Wind Cave, of Custer County, South Dakota."

CHAPTER XI

WIND CAVE CONTINUED.

PEARLY GATES AND BLUE GROTTO ROUTE.

A very much longer, more beautiful, and also more difficult journey than the one just described may be taken by those in whom the desire to see is greater than the fear of fatigue, or possibly, some little danger. With this object in view the Fair Grounds' Route is followed through Monte Cristo's Palace and into Milliner's Avenue. Here we leave it by dropping off the bridge into a rough hole, which proves to be a passage descending into Castle Garden directly beneath the Avenue, and a room of considerable size, plentifully supplied with bowlders. Although interesting to visit, it has no points of such special merit as would seem to require a detailed account, the main importance attaching to it being the fact that it is the first portion of the eighth level visited. A little beyond, however, is something quite new. The floor is covered with a light yellow crust of calcite crystal, sufficiently strong to bear the weight of a limited number of guests without much fracture. It generally gives a hollow

sound when struck, which is easily accounted
for as there are small holes noticed by which
steam evidently made its escape, and through
these cavities can be seen but they are shallow.
One place shows the crust broken up and with
the edges of the pieces overlapped, like ice broken by a sudden rise of back-water, and in
this position they have been firmly cemented.

This is where the slowly receding waters of
the cave lingered in shallow pools above the
small crevices long after the main portions had
become dry.   That the crust was formed on top
of the water, instead of beneath its surface, has
been proved by the only body of water now
standing in the cave.   This is called Silent
Lake, and being situated on another route will
be described in its proper place, but when discovered no water was visible nor its presence
even suspected until the crust gave way under
the weight of an explorer.   The thin sheet of
yellow calcite crystal thus broken was the same
as that seen in great abundance in the now perfectly dry eighth level.   The gradually decreasing volume of water has left a smooth yellow
coat on portions of the walls where irregularities or slopes were favorable, and at least one
such place is vividly remembered if once seen.
A steep incline of about fifteen feet leads to a
small oval hole through the wall; towards this
we crawled with no great ease; but getting to

the hole was far easier than going through it
into a tiny cubby not high enough to sit comfortably upright in, and too small to permit an average sized human being to turn around. Close on
the left it is shut in by another wall pierced by
two holes similar to that just passed, and each
revealing a miniature chamber scarcely more
than three feet in either direction and eighteen
inches high. Being directed to examine the
ceiling of the first, it was done with some difficulty and much satisfaction, for there in the
center was a most exquisite bit of art work, a
circular disk of "drusy" quartz about twelve
inches in diameter and having the appearance
of a flat rosette of fine black lace, in open pat-
tern with small diamonds thickly strung on every
thread; a brilliant, sparkling mass of gems.
After Mr. McDonald had carefully removed a
geode from the other little chamber, he slid
down into a fourth, the last of the diminutive
suite, having sufficient height to allow a sitting
posture with raised head, and opened the small
jewel case, while I examined the place it came
from. Here all was calcite crystal heavily
massed in various forms, and a harmony of blue
and brown, with half a dozen round, unbroken,
perfect geodes hanging from the ceiling like
oriole nests. The geode taken proved on
opening to be especially fine, being filled with
pearly white calcite crystals of both the dog-

tooth and nail-head forms, and was kindly
presented to be added to the collection of cave
specimens already purchased in town, to which
were also added handsome pieces of "drusy"
quartz, cave coral, and tufa and mineral wool.

Following the guide I now slipped down into
the larger nook just vacated, and saw with considerable chagrin that the next step was down a
perpendicular wall more than ten feet in height,
facing a high, narrow fissure, the floor of which
was merely two shelves sloping to an open space
along the middle, almost two feet wide, with the
darkness of continuing crevice below. Further
progress seemed absolutely impossible. All
things are, however, possible to those who will,
and it had been willed to pay a visit to the
grandest portion of Wind Cave. In order to
do so the descent must be made and was. Then
some little distance must be traveled along the
crevice, but the angle of elevation taken by
both sides of the bisected floor served as a sort
of prohibitory tax together with the calcite paving, since to maintain an upright position on
such a surface would require long training of a
certain professional character. That difficulty,
too, was overcome by placing a foot on either
side of the open crevice; the first consideration,
of course, being safety and not grace.

We now came to the enjoyment of the reward
of merit. Flooded with the brilliant white

light of magnesium ribbon, the crevice walls
could be seen drawing together at a height of
sixty-five feet, and both composed entirely of
larger box work than any seen before and very
heavily covered with calcite crystal, colored a
bright electric blue and glowing with a pearly
lustre. This is the Centennial Gällery, and
leaving it with reluctance we passed on into the
Blue Grotto to find it finer still. It is somewhat wider and higher, while even the extremely rough, uneven floor shows no spot bare
of heavy box work of a yet deeper blue.

The wonderful beauty of this Blue Grotto
necessarily stands beyond comparison because
in all the known world there is nothing like it.
The forms of crystal are chiefly aragonite.

From here we pass to the "Chamber de Nor-
cutt," which would be considered a very handsome room if it had no superiors: and the same
can be said of Union College, in which, however,
is the Fan Rock to claim special notice; an
immense piece of fallen box work shaped like a
lady's fan half opened.

An imposing vestibule leads into the extensive
but rather dreary Catacombs, from which we
crawled through a little hole into the M. W. A.
Hall, emerging at the top of a steep but not
high slope covered with the smooth yellow crust
of calcite encountered at other places, and in
trying to make a dexterous turn so as to go down

feet first, the descent was accomplished with
uncalculated suddenness and an unsought but
liberal collection of bruises. This, however,
was not a happening of the unexpected and
could have no attention amid scenes of wonder
and beauty, and we were close to the Geysers.
From a scientific point of view this is the most
important portion of the cave, for here is an
indisputable proof that the water in the cave
was hot and that it was subject to geyser action.
The surrounding region is covered with the
crust already described, and at the top of a gentle elevation is thrown up in the unmistakable
form of geyser cones; there being two near
together on the surface described, with a third
visible through one of these on a slightly lower
level, this one being a new discovery, as it had
escaped observation until we called attention to
it.

These small cones show that after the degree
of heat and the volume of water had become
reduced to the merest fraction of their former
greatness, they continued their accustomed
work here in the depth of the earth long after
the once grand old geyser had ceased to show
an outward sign of life. When the water finally became so reduced even here that the steam
could no longer force it through, or to these
latest vents, the last rising vapors fringed their
edges with a beautiful snow-white border of

crystallized carbonate of lime as fine and soft as a band of swan's down, which it resembles. In the pure, still atmosphere of the eighth level, almost five hundred feet beneath the entrance, this silent proof of ancient action will endure for the admiration and instruction of many generations yet to come. Few mortals will ever be honored with memorials so lasting or so convincing of vanished power.

Proceeding on the journey the next chamber is the A. O. U. W. Hall, a large, irregular room, by the rise of which a return to the seventh level is accomplished; and the next entered is the Tabernacle, not at all resembling the last, although a similar description would be correct.

Now is reached what many consider the cave's greatest charm, The Pearly Gates. And marvelously beautiful it certainly is.

Approaching by a slightly lower level, we see a gateway opening between large rocks that light up with the soft lustre and varied tints of mammoth pearls. A wonderful effect is produced by the white calcite crystal spread in unequal thickness over the dark surface of the encrusted rocks. Just without the gate is a short but not golden stairway leading to it, and immediately within is the Saint's Rest, a chamber of moderate size beautified by another great rock on which are combined the warm, pearly glow of calcite and the cold glitter of

frost by the later addition of lime carbonate
vapor-crystals to the calcium carbonate aragonite.

Next beyond is the chamber containing the
Standing Rock behind which Mr. Johnstone
made his famous discovery of the concealed pin-
head. It is an immense great fallen rock on
whose dark surface are scattered transparent
flake-like crystals of satin spar, resembling
the congealed drops of a summer shower.
The mind-reader entered the chamber by the
way we shall leave it.

Returning to the spot from which the Pearly
Gates were first viewed, we stand facing the
most beautiful of this imposing group of brilliant
scenes, The Mermaid's Resort. This is a small
cove with wave marks in the white beach sand,
above which rises a projecting, sheltering cliff
as purely white as freshly fallen snow, with a
fine deposit of frost work in thick moss-like
patterns two and three inches deep.

This crystalline mass, so white and fragile,
has to perfection the appearance of hoar-frost
about a steam-vent in extremely cold weather,
and was, no doubt, formed in a somewhat similar manner. It is crystallized carbonate of lime,
and could have been deposited in such extremely
delicate forms only by the heavily charged
vapors rising from hot water. No one needs to
be told that hot water will take and hold in

solution a much larger quantity of solid matter than is possible to cold water, with all other conditions the same; nor is it news that a portion of the solid substance is carried off in the rising steam. Now the geyser cones, so recently visited on the next lower level, prove both the heat of the water and its heavy charge of solids, which gave it a far more intense heat than pure water could have equaled, and this in turn drove the steam to greater distances than otherwise it would have reached. , When cooled to such a point as to be reduced to a light vapor, its movement was checked by various walls, projections, and ceiling as were in its upward path, and these received the minute particles of burden, while the somewhat brisk motion of the atmosphere, occasioned at these points by the mixing of that of higher temperature from below with the lower from above, is responsible for the dainty and varied forms assumed by the fragile structure.

Once more resuming the journey, we admire the rugged charms of University Heights, a somewhat larger and higher room than the next, St. Dominic's Chamber, but perhaps not more interesting than the Council Chamber, which besides other attractions is to some extent also a Statuary Hall. From the Council Chamber the Alpine Way leads up into the Fair Grounds directly above. This Alpine Way is a sort of cork-screw twisting through the rocks, not unlike a badly walled well, assisted at the lowest portion by a short and nearly pe. pendicular ladder. Next is the Assembly Room, or Crown Chamber, as it is also called on account of a handsome crown conspicuously placed. This room also contains a Moose so perfectly carved that the skeptic who searches diligently for imperfections finally clamors for the whole company to celebrate his discovery of the artist's noble skill.

Leaving this room we re-enter Milliner's Avenue and soon cross the bridge from which, a few hours ago, we decended into the eighth level by way of Castle Garden; and now the return to the surface is by the route followed before, and we arrive there at last terribly weary, but more than well pleased.

TOP OF GLACIER.
Page 155.

CHAPTER XII.

GARDEN OF EDEN, THE GLACIER, AND ICE PALACE.

There is yet another long and charming line of travel open to those who have sufficiently steady heads and light feet to suffer no loss of confidence or depression of spirit when mounting the steep stairway whose limit seems lost in the dark distance above.

There being but the single entrance, a repetition of the worn and ancient statement that all roads lead to Rome, means that many journeys may be taken in Wind Cave, but all must have the same beginning.

In the tourist season the guides have not time during the day to bring out specimens to supply the demand, so on this account night trips are of frequent occurrence; and on these occasions the number of persons in all that vast space seldom exceeds half a dozen, but their voices and laughter, and the blows of their hammers, can be heard at greater distances than would seem possible, and give an agreeable sense of companionship; yet the voice does not travel by any means so far as in other caves.

The evening we were to make the long trip just mentioned, our guide being ready before any others had gone in, we started the advance on the ninety-seven miles of enclosed, unoccupied space and had almost reached the level of the Bridal Chamber when he remembered a forgotten and necessary roll of magnesium ribbon, for which it was needful to return to the office in the upper building. I sat down on the lowest step of the great stairway to wait, and for a very short time was entirely alone in the largest cavern in the world, excepting the Mammoth Cave of Kentucky.

The unexpected experience seemed suddenly to become one of the great events of a lifetime, and was unmarred by the disturbing apprehensions of any possible danger. The entire absence of sound was indescribably awe-inspiring as

"Strata overleaping strata from the center
    to the crust,
Rose, Alp-high, in molten silence, as the
    dead rise from the dust;"

but the feeling of complete isolation from the living world would not require an unlimited time to merit the one word—horrible. Even some peril with ample companionship would be more agreeable, while it is a curious fact that the combination of companionship with silence is charming. On the occasion of one visit to the cave it was painful to observe the actual suffering of a lover of quiet, from the good-natured, but heedless, chatter of two of the party.

Presently steps on the stairs broke the stillness, a glimmer of light pierced the intense darkness that surrounded the circle of one candle, and the upper world seemed not so far away.

The interrupted journey was resumed, the route being that already described as far as the Confederate Cross Roads, where, this time, we go straight on in the main fissure instead of turning into the cross-crevice, as was done before.

We were overtaken by the specimen party and recognized the three laughing young girls only by their voices, as in full suits of overalls and white duck caps, they looked like boys. Those who reside near the large caves have overcome their objection to this costume, as it gives much greater freedom and ease of movement, besides being a decided economy. Feminine garments are so easily destroyed, but for artistic effect the substitute cannot conscientiously be recommended.

Beyond the Cross Roads the first chamber is Breckinridge Gallery, a long, rambling hall in which are combined the attractions already passed and those yet to come, but having no striking feature predominating to give special character other than the grandeur of extreme roughness, which is also the quality most observed on passing into the Stone Quarry, where great accumulations of blocks seem waiting preparation for shipment.

The next " open country " is protected from public trespass by the Garden Wall, which appears to have been well built in the long ago by masons properly trained in their craft, and extends, at a uniform height, to the Fallen Flats, where the floor is covered with slabs of enormous size that have fallen from the ceiling since water occupation ceased, as is clearly shown by the sharp edges and surfaces entirely unworn.

The journey now becomes more interesting as the Cliff-Climbers' Delight is reached, and we go steadily up the long flights of stairs until visions of St. Peter begin to rise and we wonder which way the key will turn. Near the top is a handsome growth of snow-white mold hanging in long draperies behind the ladder or spread like an asparagus fern flattened against the rock.

Arrived at the top limits of the stairs the ascent is by no means finished, but continues through three large chambers known as Five Points, the Omaha Bee Office—named by one of the staff of that well known journal—and the W. C. T. U. Hall, dedicated to the service of the organization by one of its workers.

At last the upward journey is ended at the Silent Lake in the first, or highest, level. This, as has already been observed, is the only body of water now standing in the cave, and is not more than ten feet long by six in width and twelve inches deep. The scanty volume is maintained by the very limited inflow of acidulated percolating water which reaches the small receiving basin charged with calcium carbonate; and being cold, the charge is being precipitated on the bottom instead of forming a crust over the surface as in former times when the controlling influence was a degree of heat sufficient to sustain solid matter without disturbing motion.

Rising above the Silent Lake is the Glacier, its moist surface suggesting that the lake is fed by a slight thaw, while the perpendicular front at the water's edge gives the impression of a berg having recently broken off and floated away.

The Glacier flows between two high walls of dark rock, and the steep incline of perhaps seventy feet, covered with a smooth deposit of calcite and shining with moisture, has the appearance of ice and is as uninviting for a climb. The top is connected with the roof above by a group of short, and for this region, heavy columns of dripstone, the oldest formation of that character in the cave.

An occasional overflow of the lake passes out

to one side, then turns and goes under the Glacier where its first few feet of descent are called the Pearl Beds, where a variety of water-polished pebbles are being coated over and cemented together with calcite crystal.

From the Glacier down to the lowest level of the cave by another route than that taken for the ascent, there is abundant evidence that at one time this portion of the cave was subject to excessively violent activity, and if studied with a view to the penetration of the principle of geyser action, offers many interesting and valuable suggestions that can be added to and expanded into definite theories in connection with the balance of the cave; all important requirements are clearly shown.

At a short distance from the Glacier is a small circular dome, called the Picture Gallery, which evidently was shaped by water forced up from below. The descent from here takes us into the St. Louis Tunnel, a long rough passage leading down into the great Cathedral, by the still descending irregularities of which we finally reach the Garden of Eden, the objective point of a favorite tourist route, but usually approached from the opposite direction. It is a large chamber of very irregular shape, with an extremely uneven ceiling, dipping nearly to the floor and rising suddenly to distant heights, while every portion of all the varied surfaces glitters with a mass of frost work in every form it is known to have assumed; the banks of orange buds in different stages of expansion being exceptionally handsome. A portion of this wonderful room especially admired is Cupid's Alcove, where the frost is tinged with a pinkish flush from the brilliant paint clay captured in minute particles by the vapors. The whole room is a marvel of loveliness, but unfortunately visitors have wrought such noticeable damage that wire screening must be placed before the general admittance of large parties can be resumed.

Passing out and down to a lower level, by way of Jacob's Well, we find the source of that magnificent abundance of frost work to be in the Chamber of Forbidden Fruit, where a yellow calcite floor-crust indicates the surface level of water diminishing in volume by evaporation long after the upward flow had forever ceased, and from which the rising vapor ascended to decorate the Garden of Eden, just described. But since this water completely disappeared, leaving in evidence only the record-bearing crust, a percolating drip has prepared indisputable proof of the remote distance of that time by depositing on the crust great clusters of luscious fruits, chiefly cherries, which appear to have been carelessly tossed down in heaps, but are firmly fixed in place.

The onward journey continues up and down through Beacon Heights, a large chamber which imitates Rocky Mountain scenery and terminates at the Corkscrew Path which, as the name indicates, is a spiral path winding down like a great stairway against the wall of an approximately circular chamber which is perhaps the highest in the cave, and shows the most violent water-action. The plunging torrent rushed on from here to tear out the heavy rock and form the next chamber, known as Dante's Inferno, whence, its force being divided, it went more gently in various directions. And by one of these passages we now re-enter the main route of travel once more, and finally return to the face of the earth, wondering if it will be possible to so describe those wonderful scenes as to represent with even a limited degree of fairness or justice the awe-inspiring grandeur of the entire trip, or the perfection of fragile loveliness formed and preserved as by special miracles in the Garden of Eden.

One peculiarity of this great journey was that the box work, so abundant in other portions of the cave, was here conspicuously absent.

THE CRYSTAL PALACE.

Another route in Wind Cave is that to the Crystal Palace which, although the shortest, is the one most seldom taken by visitors, because of a

certain amount of difficulty and discomfort being
unavoidable. Only a portion of the great stairway below the entrance is descended, when we
abandon it and climb into a hole in the side-wall
of the narrow passage, from which point to the
end of the trip our feet prove to be merely en-
cumbrances.

The space crawled into and through widens
sufficiently in several places to form chambers
of good size, but the height of the ceiling is nowhere more than three feet and most of it only
two or even less. The rough rock floor is partly
carpeted with patches of loose moist clay, which
is the means of our becoming as grimy as tramps,
and its source is readily accounted for by an examination of the ceiling. This is easily made
while resting one skinned elbow at the expense of
the other. The word "abraded" is inadequate
where anything approaching real cave study is
attempted.

The box work of the ceiling has almost entirely lost its crystallization, and is as ready to
crumble as the enclosed clay, which is still
retained because it had not yet reached the
necessary point of deterioration to be carried
out before the great volume of water, required
for that service, retired from this high level of
the cave.

When finally reached, the Crystal Palace
proved worthy of the effort, its decoration being

entirely of dripstone and very beautiful, although on too small a scale to be compared with similar work in many caves: it is merely an attractive "extra" in Wind Cave, and not one of the important attractions that give the Cave the rank that may have a few equals but no superiors.

The first room is scarcely more than twelve feet in either direction and not quite six feet high. The glassy ceiling is thickly studded with small stalactites from two to eighteen inches in length, and mostly of the hollow "pipe-stem" variety, from which the surplus drip rests in white masses on the clean floor around a central bowl of good clear water.

Down the middle of the wall directly opposite the entrance a rushing little white cascade has congealed, and on either side just under the ceiling is a hollowed-out nook closely set with short stalactites and small columns, all pure white.

Near by but not connected is another room too well filled to permit an entrance, but a portion of the wall having been carried out a satisfactory view is not denied. Here the floor rises to within three feet of the ceiling, and the deposit is much heavier, so that many fine columns rise from bases that spread and meet or overlap. If the cave had no greater claim to notice than these small drip rooms, it would still be worthy of a visit.

The effort to secure flash-light pictures could only be considered successful because there are none better to be had.

The atmosphere of Wind Cave is marvelously fresh and pure, and possesses in a high degree the invigorating quality which in most caves renders unusual exertion not only possible, but agreeable as well. In all the chambers and passages there is little change in the quality of the air, and thorough tests with a standard thermometer showed the variations on the different levels, from the highest to the lowest, to be about 2°; but on different days the range was from 45° to 52°. This curious state of affairs some one else will have to explain.

The only forms of life ever found in Wind Cave are a small fly and the mountain rat.

While visiting the cave, every one connected with it was most kind and obliging, especially in showing those beautiful and difficult portions that few visitors are so fortunate as to see. While this is very far from being a complete description even of the parts visited, it will serve to show what a truly grand cavern is located at the south end of the Black Hills.

The elevation at Hot Springs is three thousand, four hundred feet, and that of the entrance to the cave is four thousand and forty feet. A source of disappointment in connection with Wind Cave is that its fine scenery cannot be effectively pictured

CHAPTER XIII.

THE ONYX CAVES.

Northwest of Hot Springs there is a group of three onyx caves, the distance to them being estimated at from seven to ten miles, if the party does not get lost, which is the usual fate of those who dispense with the service of a driver familiar with the country. In going, the longer way, over the hill-tops, claims a preference on account of distant views with a favorable light. When the Onyx Cave Ranch is reached its scenery is found to be charming, with an ideal log house overlooking the cañon, and itself overlooked by the rising slope of the wooded hill. The entrance to the cave is in the opposite wall of the cañon, and is covered by a small cabin, at the door of which the view demands a pause for admiration; then the party disappears down a narrow, rough, sloping passage of sufficient height for comfort to none but know the value of comparative degrees. It soon appeared, however, that personal comfort would travel only a short distance. The mud increased with every step, and in its midst was a small hole through which it was necessary to pass to the next lower level. This

hole being so small and its walls slanting, the
only way to accomplish the first half of the
descent was to sit down in the mud and slide,
stopping half way to examine a fine ledge of
beautiful striped onyx, white and a brownish
pink, the first outcrop in the cave, but in the
next level it is seen in rich abundance and variety; the colors being red, black and white,
brown in several shades and pure white. All
are handsome and of commercial quality and
hardness; and just above them is a ledge of fine
blue marble.

The next chamber is called the Bad Lands, on
account of a certain resemblance to that desolate region. The way into it is through the
Devil's Corkscrew, a most uninviting passage
because it stands on end and is about twelve
feet deep with circular, perpendicular walls dis-
couragingly free of prominent irregularities; but
careful study reveals a few available crags and
rough edges, by which the descent is made.
Fortunately the party decreased in size just
within the entrance. Climbing up into a hole
in the wall of this room, with no little difficulty,
the Aerial Lake is the reward of a breathless
upward struggle, and a satisfying one. The
Lake is very small, but under its clear surface
can be seen numerous growing deposits of calcite, while the roof of onyx gleams with a mass
of small white stalactites.

Returning again to the main route and traveling to the end of a short passage we beheld the entrance to Red Hall, a piece of rope ladder dangling half way down a perpendicular wall, the other half having no help whatever. The way was clear so far as the length of the ladder, and with trust in the future soon learned in cave work that distance was at once passed, and sitting on the very narrow ledge to cogitate on the possibility of further progress, Mr. Sidey solved the problem by suggesting, rather doubtfully, that the easiest way would be to drop off and allow him to interrupt the fall. This method had twice proved the only means of advance in Wind Cave and can be termed rapid transit.   The walls of Red Hall are of stratified limestone variegated with patches of red rock, and clay of the same gay hue.   It is the highest chamber in the cave and probably the largest. A hole in the wall at the floor level, near the entrance to the passage beyond, gives a glimpse of the cave river flowing on a slightly lower level, not over two feet below the floor we stand on.   The water is said to have a depth of fifteen feet, and a rock thrown in gave back the sound of a splash into water not shallow. Entering the passage already referred to, its dimensions decreased to a crawl and then to a squeeze, so that most of its length was taken in a very humble position, which permitted no regard to

FAIRIES' PALACE.
Page 165.

be paid to the ample mud or little pools of water
that must be serenely dragged through as if
carrying them away were an agreeable privilege.
Even a muddy passage ends in time, and at last
we gained a standing point and after a short
climb were in Fairies' Palace, a marvel of dainty
beauty, and worthy of the distasteful trip just
taken. We stood in a narrow passage that
divided the small chamber like the central aisle
of a cathedral, above which the white roof
formed a Gothic arch from which depended
countless little stalactites and draperies, while
on either side, six feet above the passage, was
a floor of onyx supporting exquisite columns of
which the highest are not more than three feet.
Only a short distance from the Fairies' Palace is
the almost equally beautiful Ethereal Hall, and
connecting the two I had the pleasure to discover a small arched passage more beautiful than
either.

Although much of the cave was still not visited, the long drive to town demanded a return
to the surface, but several stops were made on
the way to admire masses of onyx and groups of
curious forms in deposits of that fine stone.
One high, crooked chimney above the Corkscrew
is especially fine and correspondingly difficult
for a grown person weighted down with garments dripping mud and water; but Kimball
Stone, our boy friend, scampered up like a squirrel.

Two of the Onyx Caves had not been seen at all and Mr. Sidey expressed special regret on account of the latest discovery as no woman had ever yet entered it; but the sun was low in the west and the road had some dangerous points that must be passed before dark, so the reeking skirt was removed and without waiting to dry by the great fire kindled for the purpose we hurried off, promising to return if possible, and carrying treasures in specimens, besides an ancient lemon, which may not be called a fossil, since soft substances are said not to fossilize; but however that may be, this is a perfect lemon whose particles have been replaced with the lasting rock in the same way as the numerous Cycad trunks in the same region have been preserved to prove to us conclusively that formerly the region flourished under tropical conditions, and supported an abundant animal life of tropical nature and habits.

Soon after leaving the ranch, we descended by a sort of goat-trail-road into a grandly beautiful cañon, along the bed of which the road continues until it flows out as the water did in ages gone. By this time it had become quite dark, and the chill of the northwest night formed a combination with saturated clothing that cannot be highly recommended as a pleasure; but the natural chivalry which prompted our young escort to insist on lending his own coat, and his evident disappointment that the sacrifice was not allowed, afforded a pleasure that will continue.

THE WHITE ONYX CAVE.

A few days later it was convenient to return to the Onyx Cave ranch with the special object of entering the newest cave, which could be done with the assistance of seventy feet of rope. While necessary preparations were pending, a walk up the cañon was proposed. At a distance of perhaps a quarter of a mile above Onyx Cave evidence was seen of a very remarkable form of ancient life. It is not the usual few bones but is a cast in the rock of the cañon bed of an animal clothed in its flesh. The appearance of the head, neck, body and wings is preserved, but the tail and four limbs have been carried away by eroding waters which even now have not quite forsaken the cañon. The containing stratum is not seen in the cañon wall, and near the lower end of the cañon a fine white sandstone crops out beneath. We ask: " Was the cañon cut to its full depth while yet a Cretaceous sea was depositing beach-sand, and did the earliest horse, with wings, appear at the close of that period? Or, did an animal with fore limbs developed, retain its wings into Miocene time and leave record of its life in an arm of the Tertiary lake?" The body is that of a horse with wings attached to the shoulders. The head is

unlike that of a modern horse, being much
shorter and more rounded, but the parted lips
give a glimpse of the teeth of a young horse. If
only the feet could be found, I feel assured they
would prove that the three-toed horse of ancient
time, so abundantly in evidence throughout this
region, was possessed of wings and in some way
furnished the idea of Pegasus.

A few feet further down the cañon are a pair
of twisted wings that show the animal to have
perished in company with its mate, while trying
to escape from a sudden flood that rushed down
the cañon like a moving wall.

After some uneasy discussion about the means
of entering the new cave, it was finally decided
that the available rope was too short and not of
sufficient strength. This was, of course, a disappointment but not a surprise, as a very
peculiar quality in the rope used to enter caves
of this kind had come to notice before. The
peculiarity is, that a rope entirely above sus-
picion for the safety of a two hundred pound
man, at once weakens and must be condemned
when threatened with one hundred pounds of
woman's weight, yet there is an implied compli-
ment hidden somewhere about this protective
system that tends to reduce the sting of disappointment.

So it was agreed to spend the afternoon in the
White Onyx Cave, which is generally spoken of

WHITE ONYX MASSES.
Page 170.

simply as the Upper Cave because it occupies a higher level than the Onyx Cave already described, and is supposed to be an extension of the same although no connecting passage has been discovered.

The accompanying friend had not been costumed for caving, but was persuaded to accept a full suit of overalls, which needed the addition of a pick and pipe to make the picture perfect. Unfortunately a snap shot failed.

The entrance is in a perpendicular portion of the cañon wall, but a narrow path that starts some distance away and appears in eminent danger of falling off, makes most of the ascent comparatively easy; and the balance is completed by a short ladder whose rounds dip toward the cañon bed in a rather alarming manner, but this only proves the folly of giving too much heed to appearances, for it is strong and firmly fastened to the rocks.

Just within the entrance there is height sufficient for standing, but the roof descends suddenly and the walls come near together, reducing the passage to a crawl, and showing that in past times water poured in at this opening and not out as might be supposed. The first chamber entered is the Crystal Gallery, but it is so nearly filled with great masses of pure white onyx no standing room remains. Drops of water on portions of the onyx ceiling here are the only moisture remaining in this cave. When Mac's* head came in contact with the roof he called to the guide: " See here, little boy, you ought to sing out ' low bridge ' at that sort o' places, 'cause when I'm busy hunting a spot to set my foot in, I can't see what my head's coming to, and I like to mined a lot o' this rock with it."

Slowly, and with no danger and less comfort, we creep over, under and between great massive beds of the fine white crystalline rock until at length we enter the Ghost Chamber where no onyx has been deposited, but where numerous mountain rats have evidently been at home for many years, if we may judge from the enormous quantity of pine needles with which they have carpeted the floor. The walls show small box work crumbling to dust, and Ray climbed high into the chimney-like opening above our heads, but reported that it ended suddenly and had no attractions to offer.

Coming out, the way was somewhat varied, but more difficult, as the passages through the onyx beds were more irregular and more nearly closed; Onyx Hall being only a fair specimen of the marvelous results achieved here by the persistent regularity of an uninterrupted but slow drip, continued through hundreds of years.

It is surprising that in all these heavy beds

*Colored driver.

LOOKING OUT OF WHITE ONYX CAVE.
Page 171

there is no line or tint, or slightest trace of color anywhere, while the other Onyx Cave, so near as to suggest connection, has a gorgeous variety of rich coloring.

The view looking out from the entrance of White Onyx Cave is wonderfully fine, and equally so whether the rain falls or the sun shines, a timely shower giving us an opportunity to enjoy both.

Before leaving the ranch, a promise was made by Mr. Sidey to write a short description of the other cave, which he kindly did, and it is here given. He says:

"In trailing a deer I came across a hole on top of a long divide. On throwing a rock down the opening, I could hear it rattling against the walls until the sounds gradually died away, but there seemed to be no bottom to the hole, and I resolved to come again prepared and make explorations. After the snow had gone my twelve year-old son, Ray, and I, mounted on our trusty horses, Bonnie and Dee, equipped with ropes, candles, hamners and a pocketful of matches, set out to explore the new cave. It was a beautiful, bright spring morning, and after an hour's hard climbing over fallen timber and rocks, we reached the summit of the mountain. A search of half an hour revealed the opening which was barely large enough to allow me to pass through.

"Fastening our ropes securely to a stout log rolled across the chasm, we began to pay it out, and although we did not feel it touch bottom, I started down to explore, the length of the rope at least. As I descended I found the opening gradually widened out to eight or ten feet, a sort of inverted funnel-shaped hole with irregular wall but smooth and affording little footing. As I neared the bottom I saw the end of the rope was within four feet of it, so I landed on terra firma and called to Ray, 'All right, come down!'

"Lighting our candles we found ourselves standing on a mound of pure onyx, and on looking around could see we were in an immense cavern, whose walls sparkled and glittered as if studded with diamonds. Going down twenty feet we found a smooth-floored room that measured three hundred feet in length, twenty five feet in width, and thirty feet in height. The walls were solid white onyx lined or banded with pink and golden stripes. The ceiling was arched, and draped in fantastic shapes, and hung with stalactites innumerable. The room was so large and the drapery and festooning so delicate and beautiful, that we were filled with awe and could not speak for a time.

"At last we started to further explore this wonderland. On going to the farther end of the room we found a passage leading on. This we followed for a hundred feet and found the whole cavern lined with onyx and crystals clear as glass. After loading up with specimens we retraced our steps and on reaching the large room we had first entered we heard a roaring, rumbling noise. An awful noise truly, which filled us with an unknown dread.

"On approaching the entrance we saw a stream of water pouring down, completely filling the hole.

"For a moment we felt like rats caught in a trap, our only way of egress occupied by a stream of water falling straight down seventy feet, and then we wondered how long it would take to fill up the room.

"Suddenly the thought that there might be an outlet for the water gave us new hope, so we went to see and sure enough we found a natural water-course down through an opening we had overlooked. We gathered up courage once more, and thought the best thing would be something to occupy our time. So we set to work getting out more specimens and in a couple of hours the water stopped running and we were ourselves once more.

"Ray grasped the rope, which was soaking wet, and went up the seventy feet, hand over hand, like a cat. I, being heavier, found it quite different from going down. The rope played whip-cracker with me for some time and before reaching the top I was covered with bruises. But daylight never appeared so beautiful before.

"Here we found the cause of so much water. A cloud-burst had occurred on the Divide and a large portion of it had poured down the passage way to the cave.

"We found our horses patiently waiting for us and night closing in. Mounting we rode rapidly home, resolved never to venture into this cave again without leaving some one at the entrance to give warning in case of danger.

"John F. Sidey."

The first specimen taken out was given to us on our first visit to the ranch, and is pure white with a stripe of brilliant golden yellow. Having been invited to give a name to this new find it seems quite proper after reading the description of the deluge and seeing the bright bands of color, and considering the hopeful promise of future possibilities, to call it The Rainbow Cave.

CHAPTER XIV.

South Dakota can boast of yet another cave in the Black Hills that was formed by volcanic disturbance of the rocks and afterwards decorated in a manner peculiar to itself. This is Crystal Cave. It is nine miles from Piedmont in the eastern edge of the Hills, and easily visited from that point by way of the narrow-gauge road, which winds along the natural curves of the beautiful Elk Creek Cañon, whose walls are said to expose a depth of almost a mile of geological strata, although the exposure at any one point does not exceed three hundred feet.

The disappointment of not having seen this cave during the summer visit to the Hills grew as the weeks passed, and a request that the owner should send a description was answered with an assurance that it was impossible. Therefore, on Friday, November 13th, 1896, with a small nephew, Herbert A. Owen, Jr., for company, the trip was undertaken a second time to complete the unfinished mission.

The first glimpse of the Hills is at Edgemont in the early morning, but the train makes its way to the north through the heart of the uplift, twisting about the curves of the hills and clinging to the sides of a beautiful cañon whose high walls give way here and there to fine slopes densely covered with forests of pine and spruce. These look black in the distance and suggested the name of Black Hills to the Indians, who always have a reason for the names they give even to their children.

There are great tracts where fire has killed part or all of the timber but left much of it standing, while in other places nature has defied the power of fire and the hills are re-clothed with young trees. A recent storm had further beautified the region with a few inches of snow, but as the day advanced a chinook began to blow so that when Deadwood was reached, soon after noon, only the northern exposures retained an appearance of winter.

Deadwood is a most peculiar little city and very attractive in its peculiarity, being crowded snugly into a depression between a number of steep pine-wooded hills, which gives an appearance suggestive of a bird's nest securely located among the forks of a branching tree, and as is the case in a nest, business is chiefly transacted at the lowest depth of the enclosure. As the busy center of a great gold-mining region, the metropolis of the Hills, and the outgrowth of an exciting historical past, it claims and receives interesting attention. And while the whole

APPROACHING DEADWOOD.

Page 176

Black Hills region is still distinctly a man's country, it is called woman's paradise, and surely nowhere else are the daughters of Eve received with a more gracious courtesy or surrounded by an equally unobtrusive protecting care.

The streets leading up to the residences lack very little of standing on end, and the houses appear to have been hung in place by means of hooks and wire cord like pictures on a wall. The smelter has no reception day but admits visitors as if their pleasure were a guarantee of profit.

The finest scenery in the Hills is said to be that of the Spearfish Cañon, north of Deadwood, and the finest of that at the Falls, but this may be doubtful as other points are very beautiful, especially where the Burlington & Missouri Road requires a distance of seven miles to climb the cañon wall.

Piedmont being the nearest town to Crystal Cave, we took the early evening train on the Elk Horn Road and soon were located, and shocked to learn that the proprietor of the cave had started several days before to drive to Wind Cave for specimens. The cave was closed and no one there. The trip had been taken for the one purpose of exploring Crystal Cave, and a letter sent in advance to announce our coming, but the train carrying it was an hour late so he drove off without the mail.

There seemed at first nothing to be done but take the next returning train, which, under the circumstances, was objectionable. A night's rest and a telegram that had to be sent twelve miles by special messenger, improved the situation. The proprietor was unavoidably detained at Wind Cave, but secured a reliable guide, expressed me the cave keys, and has since married the " specimen " he had gone in quest of. May great happiness dwell at the cave many years!

The morning of the third day after our arrival found arrangements all complete, and soon after the train left Piedmont it entered Elk Creek Cañon, which is always beautiful, but on that morning was exceptionally so on account of a sudden change in the weather having covered every visible portion of the passing landscape with heavy frost. The trees on distant hills that ordinarily are black, were, for once, all softly white, and when the tall pines in the cañon were shaken by a breeze, they cast a shower of flakes like snow.

Here the cañon walls are in Carboniferous Limestone with a pleasing variety of color in the strata, and the erosion-carving not overdone, the most notable piece being the Knife-blade. This, at first view, appears to be a high, round tower, but the train following the curve, reveals

THE KNIFE-BLADE.
Page 178.

the fact that it is not a tower, but a thin, curved knife-blade. The sun just for one instant shone through a rift in the clouds, and added special charm to the scene.

A short distance beyond is Crystal Cave station, where the guide was waiting to take us in charge. He is an intelligent young man who has served an enlistment term in the army, is recently married, very obliging, and proud of being trustworthy.

The scenery here is most beautiful as well as grand. The cañon makes a sharp turn toward the south, and on the north opens out into another cañon of even greater beauty and higher walls, the perpendicular being three hundred feet in places. Crystal Cave is in the hill embraced by the junction curve. The natural entrance is more than two hundred feet above the cañon bed and was naturally approached from above. A short walk up the north cañon, whose name has unfortunately slipped away, was over ice and snow the chinook had failed to reach, and brought us to a long stairway against the wall, which affords a more direct approach than nature gave and is a fair test of physical perfection.

Finally a resting place is reached where the grandeur of the view can be enjoyed; and then a shorter stairway completes the ascent of the wall, but not of the hill, so there is still a con-

siderable upward walk through the forest of tall
pines all carpeted with brilliant mats of kinnikinic with its shining leaves, glowing in shades
of green and red, trying to rival the bright scar-
let berries.   The kinnikinic here resembles the
wintergreen of the east, while in the mountains
in Colorado it grows in the form of a shrub two
to three feet in height, but with no variation in
the leaf or berry.

At last perserverance is rewarded with a view
of the cave buildings and the summit of the hill
rising yet higher beyond, and tall, straight pines
swaying in the rising wind over all.

One of the two houses was entered and preparations quickly made for entering the cave, the
artificial tunnel entrance being only a little distance further on.

The door was unlocked, candle-sticks taken
from a shelf within, candles from the guide's
supply lighted, and we went forward at last,
into Crystal Cave.   At the end of the new
tunnel, a second door was passed through, which
is locked on the inside during the visiting season by the last guide to enter, in order that no
chance late arrival may enter alone and be lost.

The first room is a small one at the junction
of the natural and artificial entrances, from
which we go upstairs to the Resting Room, in
the highest level of the cave, and perfectly dry
but otherwise of no special interest.   After a

short rest here we went down stairs at the side
opposite that on which we entered, into a passage leading to the cave's first beauty, the Red
Room. As the name indicates, the walls are
vividly colored and represent the uncertain line
which separates the Carboniferous strata from
the Triassic rocks. The color is handsomely
brought out here in contrast with masses of
calcite crystal, so as to present by the combination a charmingly beautiful room, from which
we retired, feet first, down a "squeeze" to the
Bridal Chamber, where we found ourselves
perched on an irregular narrow ledge, high
up on the wall, and cherishing a private convic-
tion that exploration had met a checkmate; but
the guide reached the floor and my nephew,
Herbert, scrambled down with as much ease as
the chipmunk he had chased to the house top a
while before; so a little application settled the
difficulty and re-united the party. The room is
an artistic study in red, and the only reason for
its being called the Bridal Chamber is that the
way out is decidedly more rough and difficult
than that by which the entrance is effected; this,
however, is an observation not based on official
information.

Off to one side of this room is Lost Man's
Paradise, also in red and crystal, named in
honor of the timely rescue of one who had faced
the possibility of becoming a lost soul.

Another Fat Man's Misery, on a lower level, leads from the Bridal Chamber to the Big Dome, a large room with a fine dome-shaped ceiling from which heavy masses of crystals have fallen to the floor; and down a steep incline from here is Reef Rock, an immense fallen rock with box work on the under side, which at one time served to ornament the ceiling; and now this rock marks the beginning of Poverty Flat, a broad, low passage of great extent, that has been robbed of all its wonderful treasure of crystal and ends in a steep, rough declivity named Bunker Hill by the guides who dreaded to mount it when going out loaded with specimens. At the foot of the Hill is a bowlder of enormous size and with a pointed top, known as Pyramid Rock and giving the same name to the large room in which it stands.

Every portion of Crystal Cave has at one time been heavily crusted with calcite crystals, mainly of the dog-tooth variety, and any barren places are so either because the surface has been removed for specimens, or thrown down by the violence of an earthquake. But where the latter has been the cause of removal, the crystals have in most cases been renewed, which is amply evidenced by the fallen masses being crystallized on all sides; and these as well as most of the walls, are not covered thinly with one crust, but layer has been added to layer until the thickness is four to ten inches and often more. The ceilings that have been denuded by nature's forces during the same early period when water filled the cave were also renewed.

From the Pyramid Room a narrow fissure forms a passage to the Cactus Chamber, where there is a marvelous floor on which the crystals are in bunches like cacti, and the beautiful ceiling is the finest and most irregular unbroken mass of crystal yet seen.

Passing through a round hole known as the Needle's Eye, we enter Statuary Hall, where the latest inrush of water has eroded the sharp points from the crystals, leaving only smooth surfaces, and at the same time done much curious carving, the most conspicuous pieces of this work being a bear and the heads of an Indian and his baby.

Out from the Hall are two important routes, one down the steep incline of Beaver's Slide to The Catacombs, and another, which we followed first, is through Rocky Run, a rough and rocky pass, to a large and handsomely crystallized chamber called the I. X. L. Room, on account of those three letters, over twelve inches in height, being distinctly and conspicuously worked in crystal on a magnificent piece of box work that would weigh nearly half a ton, for which an offer of five hundred dollars is said to have been refused.

The next chamber beyond is Tilotson Hall, very large and extremely rough, and named in honor of a teacher from the Normal School, who delivered an address here that gave much pleasure to both visitors and guides.

The way to farther advance is now more difficult and through a jagged crevice of threatening appearance, but the trip is made in safety and with comparative ease, and brings us into Notre Dame, one of the largest chambers in the cave and perhaps the finest, although where so much is fine that may be uncertain. The display of box work and crystal is sufficiently gorgeous to do honor to the famous old cathedral of France, the ceiling especially being a masterpiece of the builder's and decorator's arts; but the grandest portion, which a visitor recently returned from foreign travel called The Russian Castle, on account of the magnificence of the large box work and pearly crystal masses, should rather be known as the great cathedral's crowning glory, The Altar.

Another large room, the handsome Council Chamber, is entered just as that Altar of pearl is lost to view; and from there an up-hill trip is taken through a narrow crevice to Whale Flat, which is the natural history room, with a large whale as the show specimen.

Going out from here we enter another crevice which serves as a steep stairway descending to

THE BRIDAL VEIL.
Page 187.

a lower level, and measures from top to bottom
one hundred and eighteen feet. This is called
Rip Van Winkle's Stairway, and although merely a high and crooked crack in the rock, is very
beautiful because heavily coated with crystal,
the effect being especially striking at the top
where the crystal is partly worn away and leaves
exposed patches of red rock.

At the foot of the Stairway is the first room
containing water, and is called the Gypsy Camp.
It is the most charming chamber yet visited,
with not the smallest spot of plain or common
rock visible. The ceiling, walls, floor, and
groups of fallen rocks, are all unbroken masses
of pearly calcite in crystals of varied sizes, with
here and there a patch coated over with pure
white carbonate of lime, or supporting a bunch
of fragile egg-shell, which is a thin, hollow
crust of lime carbonate, almost invariably having
the pointed form of the dog-tooth spar. And
there are also beautiful mats and banks of dainty
white carbonate flowers. While waiting here
for the guide to go in quest of the lunch we had
carelessly left behind, the time was utilized in
measuring the room, which is a small one.
The size of the cave and our limited time for
seeing it, prevented much-desired measurements
from being taken in all parts of the cave.

This room was found to be forty-eight feet
long, the irregular width varied from fourteen

to thirty feet and the height from four and one-
half to ten feet. The crystal water basin is
especially beautiful and the water so clear that
we stood looking into it with disappointment,
being thirsty and thinking it dry, until the
guide laughingly dipped and offered a cupful.
The basin is the segment of a circle rounding
beneath a massive, overhanging crystal ledge of
wonderful beauty, and is nine feet long by two
in width. This room and the Stairway into it
are alone worthy of a visit, but there is much
that is finer still.

Out of Gypsy Camp by way of Gunny Sack
Crawl, so named by the workmen who spread
gunny sacks to relieve the torture of crawling
over the beautiful floor of sharp crystals, we
enter the first chamber, where active operation
is still maintained and certain branches of the
great decorative industry of the cave may be
carefully studied. This operative chamber,
which is unnamed, would no doubt be called a
factory in the east, but in its own locality
would more likely be referred to as The Works.

The next chamber entered is Crystal Flat,
whose floor is completely covered with immense
crystal blocks, and the wonderful crystal ceiling
is exceedingly fine. But time being limited we
must pass on into the Lake Room, where is Crystal Lake, the largest body of water in the cave.
It is about thirty feet long by fifteen wide and

its greatest depth is said to be ten feet. The
water is cold and clear, and the gold fish introduced as an experiment three years ago are
said to have grown rapidly but not yet turned
white, and are not known to have become
blind.

At some little distance from Crystal Lake,
and not within the same range of vision,
although in the same room, is Dry Lake, which
to the surprise of the guide we found to be not
dry, but full of limpid water through which we
could distinctly see the delicate clusters of crystals it is depositing. They are of a pale honey
yellow and are called Gum-drops on account of
the resemblance to that variety of confection.

The name Dry Lake was given because in
blasting out a passage a misdirected shot went
through the bottom of the Lake, which in consequence was soon drained; but the heavily
charged water has sealed up the unfortunate
break, and resumed its interrupted work. The
ceiling drops to a height of little more than
three feet directly above the Lake margin, and is
a beautiful crystal mass, which at a little distance down the sloping floor appears as the
background for a fine piece of cave statuary
called The Bridal Veil, and formed of cream-
tinted dripstone. Not a great deal of imagination is required to see a slender girlish figure
completely enveloped in the flowing folds of a

wedding veil that falls lightly about her feet. The figure itself is three feet ten inches in height and stands on an almost flat circular base of the same material, that measures nine inches in depth and two feet eight inches in diameter. At times the water rises sufficiently to cover the base, in proof of which it left a fringe-like border of small sharp crystals, such as could be formed only beneath the water's surface. Most of this border has, unfortunately, been chiseled off for specimens, but will be renewed in time if left undisturbed; and that condition can easily be secured with a few feet of wire netting.

To one side of this room is a most daintily beautiful alcove so profusely decorated with fragile forms of dripstone that a passage through it without causing damage is extremely difficult. This alcove is about twenty-five feet in either direction, with a sloping floor almost covered with stalagmitic growths above the earlier deposit of sharp crystals, and many of these rise in slender columns to the glass-like ceiling, which varies in height from three to six feet and is thickly studded with small stalactites of both varieties—the pointed, solid form, and those of uniform size, which are always hollow like a pipe stem. The central ornament is the Chimes, a musical group of stalactites which is scarcely more beautiful than Cleopatra's Needle, at a

THE CHIMES.
Page 188.

THE NEEDLE.
Page 188.

distance of a few feet to one side, a transparent column four feet in height and having an average circumference of seventeen inches.

The Abode of the Fairies is a similar, though smaller room, with The Tower of Babel for a handsome show-piece. While this portion of the cave is extremely attractive, the measurements given show that in comparison with caves of other states the drip deposit here is too small to be reckoned an important feature in itself, but in conjunction with the miles of calc-spar that give the cave a character distinctly its own, it well repays all attention.

Leaving Lake Room we enter a newly opened, long, dry passage to Slab Room, where a comparatively recent earthquake has shaken down the ornamental ceiling and spread it in great slabs over the floor; and having since remained perfectly dry it has the appearance of being the work of yesterday. This room is remembered as the one in which a party of workers were lost, and one of their number gave a severe nervous shock to the junior proprietor by suggesting that as he was acting as guide and unable to lead them out, it was only right that he should be the first victim to satisfy their hunger. A rescuing party with extinguished candles was listening behind a rock to the blood-curdling speech, and came forward to restore cheerfulness.

A long, irregular, frosty looking crevice called

Jack Frost Streak, conducts us from Slab Room
and ends at Mold Ladder, on which we pause to
admire a wonderful growth of snow-white cave
vegetation, before ascending into Santa Claus'
Pass, the longest passage in the cave. It is a
rough crevice named from the fact of being discovered on Christmas Eve, and ends at the
Government Room on the main tourist route
where a U. S. pack saddle and apparently port-
able bath tub are conspicuous.

Next beyond is a very large room named New
Zealand, on account or its icy appearance and
the undisputed possession of a seal. This room
in turn opens into Mold Chamber, where an old
board platform, formerly used for the display
of specimens, has fostered the most marvelously
beautiful growth of mold: it hangs in ropes five
and six feet long, with tasseled ends, and in
broad, looped draperies; but is most beautiful
where it has taken possession of the rocks and
spreads out on the flat surface like large open
fans, with deep, soft feather borders.

Having been in the cave eight hours, we now
followed the outward passage from Mold Chamber and soon reached an open trap door where the
guide suggested to Herbert that he would be
afraid to go down alone and allow him to close
the door; but the child surprised him by quietly
stepping down and then asking why he wished

it, only to be told " because we are coming too." Which we did and found ourselves in the main entrance passage, and in due time returned to the outer world where a terrific wind was roaring through the tall pines and the early winter evening had already closed in dark.

The guide locked the cave, walked with us to the house where he lighted a lamp and left us to prepare for the return to town; but the lamp, belonging to a bachelor, was empty, so we made our preparations in imitation of the blind. On the guide's return he lighted a candle, but suggested that twenty minutes were generally allowed for reaching the station.

The house was accordingly closed and as we walked down the long, curving slope to the stairway, he told of a new and unknown bobtailed wolf that has recently made its first appearance among the hills in considerable numbers and to the terror of stock. It attacks and bites horses or cattle, and after waiting for the fatal poison inflicted to take effect, falls to and eats the victim.

The uncovered platform which serves as a station being reached a few minutes before the train arrived, I expressed an unwillingness to detain our guide longer on account of his having a walk of four and a half miles to his home; but he declined to consider the subject;

saying he had been directed not to leave us until we were taken safely on the train, which came sweeping round the curve on time and stopped for us.

TOWER OF BABEL.
Page 189.

CHAPTER XV.

According to agreement the guide again met us at the station on the following morning, for another day in the cave, which we entered with no unnecessary loss of time, and hurrying through the main entrance passage, Government Room and Statuary Hall, went down Beaver Slide, which, on the previous day, we had passed to enter Rocky Run. Our descent into the crevice took us past those portions known as Suspension Bridge and Rebecca's Well, and over some very "rough country" to the most wonderful parts of the cave. Numerous passages open out in various directions; one to rooms of frost work of great beauty; another to the Ribbon Room where the drip deposits on the walls are in ribbon-like stripes of red, yellow, and white, while others yet are ways to the Catacombs. And it is the Catacombs we particularly wish to see, as they most perfectly represent the individual character of the cave and have, as yet, received no injury from either time or man; but is a region as difficult to travel as the way of the transgressor, and many miles

can be traversed with no prospect of coming to
the end. But where locomotion is so slow and
painful, the owner of a pedometer would find
that instrument a discouraging companion and
soon learn better than to consult its record pub-
licly.

The Catacombs are a series of connected fissures and small crevices in which every inch
of exposed surface is covered with clear, trans-
lucent, almost transparent, calcite crystals,
neither coated with lime nor stained with clay;
nor even is the pearly lustre dimmed with the
slightest trace of dust. The crystals are very
sharp and of all sizes, ranging from half an inch
to three and a half inches in length, the larger
sizes being conspicuously abundant. The entire region is an enormously large, perfectly
formed, and undamaged geode. In reality, the
whole cave is a great cluster of connected geodes, and a similar work probably does not exist, but if it does, has never been discovered.
The fissures from which it is formed were
opened by volcanic violence and then enlarged,
and afterwards decorated by the varied power
of water, in action or repose.

When the storms toward the close of the Tertiary period suddenly overwhelmed with floods
the dense growth of tropical vegetation and
multitudinous animal life in the Northwest,
the waters necessarily became heavily charged

with the naturally resulting carbonic acid gas, and this, acting on the limestone rocks, would decompose them, leaving a residual clay and taking the chief portions of the mineral components in solution, to be afterwards deposited according to circumstances and conditions; and these are indicated by the various results found in Wind Cave, Crystal Cave, the Onyx Caves and the Bad Lands. The latter being previous to that time by no means "bad," but richly luxuriant in tropical vegetation, which gave shelter from the heat to great numbers of curious animals.

Some approximate idea of the extreme age of these caves may be gained from the fact that bones of a three-toed horse have been discovered in a chamber of Crystal Cave that must be practically unchanged since the remains were carried in from the outside, as otherwise they would have been buried beneath the fallen masses of crystal covered rock with which the entire floor is cumbered. And yet this room is so remote from any present connection with the outer world that it is impossible for their introduction to have taken place in recent times.

In the beautiful Catacombs progress is as slow as in a cactus thicket or a blackberry patch. The crevices lack none of the usual crevice irregularities; high places must be mounted or descended, chasms crossed and narrow passages crawled through, while extra caution must be exercised to avoid striking the head or making a misstep that might result in a fall. The hands are in constant use and soon become so sensitive that holding a soft handkerchief gives infinite relief; but the worst experience is the "crawls" where only the soles of the feet, being temporarily turned up, seem safe from the savage treatment of the sharp calcite dog-teeth. The worst crawl encountered was a small one having a downward slope with a jump-off at the end which necessitated its being taken feet first. Fortunately it was short. But in no place do the difficulties outweigh the pleasure of beholding scenes of such beauty, or suggest regret for the time, torn garments, and personal exertion required for its enjoyment.

In many portions of the cave the surface layer of crystals has had the points worn away by the action of water, later than that in which they were formed; but in the Catacombs and other extensive regions as well, the finished work of crystallization is preserved in an absolutely perfect condition. And everywhere the largest crystals are on the under side of a projection or the roof of a cavity.

As the day was passing far too rapidly and many points of special interest yet remained unseen, we turned with reluctance from the beauty and relief from the hardships of exploration in the Catacombs, and made our way over a crevice into Santa Claus' Pass, which was traversed for a considerable distance and then abandoned for a low crawl terminating at the Senate Chamber. This is a large room extending to Poverty Flat, and is brilliantly red and purely white, most of the crystal presenting a smooth surface. Under the Senate Chamber there is said to be some fine box work which we had no time to visit. The name of this chamber was given by a visiting party composed of members of both houses of Congress. A smaller room, which is really an extension of the Senate Chamber, has handsome walls of white and red box work on account of which the same distinguished party called it the Senate Post-office.

From here a difficult crawl, through red rock, well-worn by the action of water, leads to the Starr Chamber, another large room in white and red, and named by Senator Starr of South Dakota.

Opening out from the last room is a curious, dangerous looking, narrow, crevice-chamber known as Suicide Room on account of the threatening appearance of over-hanging rocks, some of which have at times fallen in great masses of various sizes to form an irregular floor; and a descent of this is necessary in order to reach a short and extremely rough crawl, beautifully and painfully decorated with sharp crystals above and below and on the sides. From this

we emerge into Rainy Chamber, an elliptical
room not less than two hundred feet long by
one hundred feet wide, with a tent-like ceiling
rising high in the center and sloping down to
meet the floor, which also slopes irregularly
toward a deep central depression, giving the
room a greater height than any other visited.
The high points are generally seen in the narrow crevices, while the rooms of generous
length and breadth are usually low, many of
the largest having an average of five feet or
even less.

Although there is frequent intersection of
crevices, and each chamber has passages leading
out on every side, the general direction of the
cave is said to be northwest-southeast.

Rainy Chamber is named from the fact that
during the early months of summer water falls
constantly in the form of a light shower; but it
drips at all times, and in consequence there is an
opportunity to study the active process of formation of one of the deposits which is very
abundant in Wind Cave and considered the
most perplexing. This is the pop-corn, and the
theories of its origin have been steadily rejected
at Wind Cave because of a doubt being entertained as to whether it has been deposited under
water or by drippings. Here in Rainy Chamber
it is fully explained. Near the center of the
room the fallen masses are heavily crystallized,

much of the groundwork being fine box work and the crystals in perfect condition. On these crystals the pop-corn is being formed, and specimens can be seen in all stages of development, from the beginning to an approximate degree of finish; and whatever the position it occupies on the receiving surface, either on top, underneath, or on a side exposure, it always maintains the same relative position as growing plants on the mundane sphere. The water falling on the upper surface in scattering drops forms myriads of minute stalagmites; on side positions the falling drop first strikes the point exposed to its line of descent and then spreads. The scant moisture slowly makes its way down sloping sides and shelving edges, leaving on each small irregularity a tiny portion of its volume, to deposit an infinitely small charge of solid substance, and the balance finally hangs in moisture less than drops on the growing grains of the under surface.

Pop-corn, therefore, is the globular aragonite of the stalagmitic variety. A small specimen from Rainy Chamber, placed beside one of the same color from Wind Cave, shows them to be absolutely alike.

Rainy Chamber is the room in which the bones of the three-toed horse, already referred to, were found, but their presence has not yet been explained; therefore the case is open to con-

jecture and several theories may be advanced
and their values considered.   The first question
when such a discovery is made, is whether the
living animal was possibly a cave-dweller; which,
as the horse was not, is quickly disposed of and
attention turned to the next, the possibility of a
carniverous animal having carried his prey into
the dark recesses of the cave in order that the
enjoyment of his dinner might be undisturbed.
This theory is equally unavailable by reason of
the topographical features presented.   If the
present natural entrance to the cave were the
only way into this room from the outside, the
distance was too great and beset with many
difficulties; besides which the final passage is
too small to admit an animal of sufficient size to
carry any considerable portion of even a very small
horse.   But if at that period the room had
direct communication with the outside through
an opening since closed, the shape of the walls
indicate that it must have been a pot-hole in the
roof, and through this an animal could have
entered by falling, which the horse and others
may have done. .But it seems most probable
that the remains were carried in by the water
through such a hole before it was closed at the
beginning of the Quaternary period, when the
erosion of the Hills was most active.

Rainy Chamber also contains a large and

beautiful assortment of the small polished and coated pebbles called cave pearls.

The guide being anxious that we should not fail to see the Niagara Room, we now turned toward a low, broad opening in the wall, a short distance to the right of the entrance, where the rising floor and descending ceiling, failing to meet, had overlapped; so we made our way up a steep, smooth bank, and then down on the other side over a broken, rocky surface for a distance of about twenty feet, when the roof at last joined the floor and two small water-worn holes at the point of junction revealed an untempting passage within. The broader of these holes was three feet, but too low to be considered an entrance; the other was round but certainly not so large as our guide, who was preparing to enter it with doubts of his ability to make the trip, on account of having increased in size since his one entrance there, on which occasion two smaller guides pulled him through the tightest places. Carefully comparing his size with that of the hole he sat beside, there was no possibility of doubt that if the attempt were made he would stick fast, and that would place our little party in dire straits. Consequently I insisted that it should not be, but he was unwilling that Niagara should be missed when so near. Finally I positively refused to go unless he would consent to give us instructions and remain where he was

while we went without him, to which he at last
yielded with extreme unwillingness. He had
frequently shown us the guide's marks, and now
earnestly cautioned me to advance only as they
point, and turn back if they should fail.

The small nephew went on a reconnoitering
expedition to the end of the passage, and
reported that the jump-off there was higher than
himself but he could get down. I now crawled
through the hole and found the passage to be a
"crawl" or rather a "sprawl," from fifteen to
eighteen inches high, but having an ample width
varying from three to six feet. The smooth,
straight floor has a steep downward inclination
and is thickly covered with dust.

Having reached the widest portion, which is
rear the end, Herbert directed me to turn, so as
to come down the jump-off feet first, where
there was a little difficulty in landing, as the
perpendicular wall, which proved to be almost
five feet high, offered only one projecting
help, and that within a few inches of the
base; but in obedience to his advice to "reach
one foot a little farther down and then drop,"
I advanced the right one, to be told not that,
but the other, and was soon down where it was
possible to observe with interest that the right
foot had been swinging above an open fissure.
We stood in a wide crevice running at right
angles to the obnoxious passage we had just

quit, and immediately found a guide's mark on a large rock, and others followed at intervals of a few feet over extremely "rough country" as the guides say. Everywhere the work of water was apparent, not in the crystal deposits of still water as in other portions of the cave, but the erosion due to its rushing through. Carefully following the marks, they led into a cross-crevice that took us under Rainy Chamber, and ends there by widening into a circular chamber of about fifty feet width in either direction, and rising to a height of nearly fifty feet in a fine dome. Down the wall from near the top of the dome there appears to flow a beautiful waterfall showing a variety of colors in the straight lines, as if from refraction. The fall is, of course, dripstone, and I knew we had found Niagara, although we had gone beyond the reach of the guide's voice almost at the start. A huge rock directly under the dome has received the falling drip until it represents a mountain cataract. These deposits testify to the great age of the chamber they adorn, as they were necessarily not commenced until all heavy flow ceased, and in Crystal Cave the accumulation of dripstone is so slow that it is said six years' observation can detect no increase whatever.

Several small passages at the floor level gave exit to the great volume of water that evidently at one time entered this crevice, from Rainy Chamber, by the route we followed, and being checked in its course the lower end of the crevice became filled, under pressure; and the low position of the outlets gave this water a whirling motion that in time excavated the dome-shaped room.

No part of Crystal Cave has ever been occupied by a river, but its fissures, opened by the violence of earth movements accompanying nearby volcanic disturbances, have been filled more than once by the inrush of waters which repeatedly submerged the whole Black Hills region.

Following again the marks which guided us into Niagara Room, we soon came within hailing distance of a voice expressive of profound relief; and as we crawled up the sloping passage, over-heated and breathless with the exertion, the guide assured us he was most truly thankful to see us again, as he had never in his life experienced so severe a scare as since it had occurred to him that we had gone beyond the limits of communication without a single match.

He also said I had been where no lady had ever gone before, and took satisfaction in the fact that many men have refused to make the venture with a guide.

Leaving this portion of the cave, by returning as we came, through Suicide Room, Starr Chamber, and Senate Chamber, we crawled along the rocks overhanging a narrow fissure, to reach a ladder at the end, by which we descended to another part of the Catacombs. Here, after traveling a long distance over uneven floors covered with sharp crystals, as were all surfaces, through large, low rooms, and narrow, crooked passages, constantly assisting the difficult advance with our hands, like monkeys, we finally came to The Grotto, which is probably the most remarkable room in this very remarkable cave. It is a large room, with much of the irregular ceiling so low that even the small nephew struck his head severely while turning to warn me, as he often did, of threatening inequalities in the floor and light them with his own candle. The crystals here are exceptionally fine, being very sharp and of unusual size, besides many of them being double—that is, pointed at both ends. Through this beautiful ceiling there is a percolating drip adding stalactites to the crystal-points and piling stalagmites on the crystal masses below, varying this with imitation cascades, mats of small flowers, and masses of pop-corn. Off to one side in a kind of recess there is a depression in the crystal floor filled with clear, cold water.

A glance at the time now showed us to be in danger of failure to meet the train to town, and consequently, tired as we were after nine hours of rough travel and much climbing, it was

necessary to make our way out with more speed
than comfort, and we found the weather turning
very cold. The cave was carefully locked,
preparations for the train hurriedly made, the
house closed, and as we left it the train could be
heard coming down the cañon, but we arrived
at the station first, though breathlesss, and a few
minutes later were in Piedmont, too tired to
properly enjoy a hot venison supper.

As to the size of Crystal Cave, it is impossible
to make any positive statement; for as Mr.
McBride, the proprietor, says, no survey has
yet been made. Other persons said that thirty-
six miles is the greatest claim made for the
combined length of all passsages, and sixteen
miles the least, so it may be wise to accept the
lesser number until a survey proves it wrong.

The box work in Crystal Cave is not of such
great abundance as to demand special attention,
but is very beautiful, and one variety deserves
particular mention. These boxes have been
formed in dark red sandstone, and after being
emptied of their original contents, have been
completely filled with colorless calcite crystals,
and over this is spread an outer surface of the
same crystals tinted a brilliant flame color by
red paint-clay having been taken in solution by
the crystal forming waters. A specimen of this
was a temptation too great to be resisted even in
the owner's absence.

Some of the box work is of such size that a single box may have a capacity equal to that of a bushel measure, but it is less beautiful than the smaller forms.

On the following morning we left Piedmont, and having a desire for greater personal knowledge of the Hills, took the same train which had taken us to the cave, and traveled to its western terminus, Lead City. The interesting scenery makes this a desirable trip for any one visiting the Hills, but its beauty is chiefly massed at the ends, the middle distance being over gradually rising ground, which is without a counterpart of the rocky cañon left behind or more than a suggestion of the high hills yet to come. The special charm of this portion was the magnificent pine forest which covered it until three years ago, when it was swept by a terrible fire, from which the settlers escaped with only their lives; and even that would have been impossible if the railroad company had not kept refuge trains waiting for them just ahead of the flames. The prominent geological feature here is the porphyry dikes, which are becoming more numerous and more prominent, and in many places resemble a conspicuous group near Harney Peak, called The Needles. These dykes are of special interest in connection with a study of the caves, since they are probably of simultaneous origin. The same volcanic movements that caused the violent upheaval of the whole region, and thrust up molten masses through the strata to form a central core to the Hills, must also have rent the nearby regions with fissures through which probably much gas escaped, and having been further opened and then adorned, now demand our attention as caves of unique and curious beauty.

The approach to Lead is over the hill-tops with a magnificent distant view, and the first glimpses of that young city famous for having as a center the Homestake mine, the largest gold mine in the world, are charming. It is situated far down in a valley among the high hills and spreads some distance up the surrounding slopes.

The works of the great mine are wonderful, and visitors welcome to examine whatever they find interesting; any questions they wish to ask are graciously answered, although every one is busy. This is not a special favor to the exceptional few, but the courtesy shown to all. Visitors are also welcome to descend into the mine, but as an attendant is necessary on account of dangers to be avoided, a permit must be obtained at the office.

Several other caves have been discovered in the Black Hills, the largest of which is the Davenport Cave at Sturgis. Very little exploration has yet been done in it, but indications are said to be that it will take rank among the large ones.

At Galena, a new mining town of golden promise, there is reported to be an Ice Cave, where ice forms at all seasons, and during the warm weather is a source of comfort and pleasure to the miners.

In the evening, as train time for continuing the homeward journey approached, the snow storm which began gently early in the afternoon, grew steadily more severe. A carriage to the depot was not to be had, as every vehicle in town had gone to the funeral of an old-timer in the Hills and the return delayed by the storm. The situation could not be regarded as a special pleasure, but cave hunters learn to accept whatever is and be thankful for the general average. At the last moment, however, a team was driven up and permission given us to make use of it. It proved to be the private conveyance of the hotel proprietor, and the young boy who accompanied us, his son.

Our train was on time, and the ride through the Hills to their southern limit, in the falling snow, was wonderfully beautiful; but the storm continued for many days and was one of the most severe on record.

Those persons who have been so unfortunate as to permit themselves to accept a ready made opinion of dangers and roughness to be met with in the more newly settled regions, might find a tour of the Hills doubly interesting by making a supplementary study of "The Living Age," which cannot be so correctly viewed from a distance as is sometimes supposed, since the specimens exhibited are not always a true average of the strata they are supposed to represent.

CHAPTER XVI.

CONCLUSION.

After a visit to the marvelous caverns of the Black Hills, much may be added to the pleasure already enjoyed, through the explanatory activity of the Yellowstone National Park, where even the wonderful combinations of beauty and grandeur are by no means the full measure of attraction and charm. Here is found evidence to verify theories concerning the caves, and those theories in turn contribute in no small degree to a satisfactory understanding of the mysteries of geyser action. For scientific study the two regions should be taken together, since the natural conditions are practically the same, and the chief difference lies in the stages of development; the present of the Park explaining the recent past of the Hills, while the present of the Hills foretells the future of the Park. It seems that Nature, with a full appreciation of the limits and restrictions binding our powers to penetrate certain secrets of an intermittent force, has in this great western country carefully prepared what might quite properly be termed a progressive course of study, wherein each locality makes plain a special point that somewhere else appears obscure.

As has been said in the preceding chapters, the two great caves in the Black Hills of South Dakota cannot be accounted for by the same methods as are recognized as being responsible for the slow excavation of the best known caves of the United States. Although there is every indication that both these caves have been subject to the action of enormous volumes of water, there is equally positive evidence that neither was ever the scene of a flowing cave-river. The lowest levels in both show the narrowest fissures and the heaviest deposits of crystal, by which we infer that the water was held in confinement here, while all the higher passages or channels bear witness to the water's flow. But many of these channels in Crystal Cave, or indeed' we might say, most of them, present an unmistakable record of the gauge of the water stage at different periods. During the earlier time, when the volume of water and consequent pressure were greatest, frictional motion must have been limited to the main channel connecting with the vent, and the high gauge of water maintained a fairly uniform degree of heat near its surface. In consequence of these conditions geyser action, probably, was constant, and chemical activity was such that great chambers were formed and then decorated, as already described, with wonderful masses of crystal. As the water gauge receded to lower levels the higher chambers became storage basins for water and steam forced up by the pressure from below, and the time required for these to fill and accumulate sufficient pressure to continue the ejectment, formed the periods between eruptions after the geyser became intermittent. It was during this stage that the sharp crystals in many of the channels, now called passages, were worn down to smooth surfaces; and later, when water occupied only the lowest level, and the great geyser had become reduced to merely a steam vent, the channels immediately connecting with that level were in their turn subjected to the same smoothing process, and then all action ceased.

As no two of the glorious geysers of the Yellowstone Park are alike, neither do the two great caves of the Hills indicate that they should be so. The vent-tubing of each is quite unlike that of the other in all the essential governing points of length, size, shape, angle of inclination and power-conserving bends. And the differences extend in an almost equally marked degree throughout the vast and complicated succession of storage chambers and their connecting channels. The small vent of Wind Cave shows that the ejected jet was far from being equal to that of the Crystal Cave in volume; but the nearly perpendicular long arm of its tube shows also that its jet attained a much greater height, even supposing that it should be necessary to make some allowance for a short elbow at the top.

Dr. Hayden's geological party gave much attention to the Yellowstone Park while its wonders were new to the world, and observations were made at various times during the period included between the years 1869 and 1870. The special study, and full report of the geysers became the duty of Dr. A. C. Peal, whose descriptions and conclusions were published in U. S. Geological Survey Report, 1878, Part II. In the final pages of his report he quotes the leading authorities on geyser action, and applies the principles of their theories, according to his own judgment, to the geysers of the park. Since copies of this report are not now easily obtained, nor even always accessible to the increasing number of personages who visit the park, it may be well to quote from him some of the theories he discussed and the opinions he expressed. On page 416, beginning the chapter with the derivation of the word geyser from the Icelandic word *geysa*—to gush, he continues:

"We now come to the definition of a geyser. It may be defined to be a periodically eruptive or intermittent *hot* spring, from which the water is projected into the air in a fountain-like column. The analogy between geysers and volcanoes has frequently been noticed and the former have often been described as volcanoes which erupt heated water instead of melted lava. We have italicized the word hot in the definition just given, because springs containing a large amount of gas may simulate geysers.

"The difference between geysers and ordinary hot springs is not readily explained, nor even always recognized. The difference between a quiet thermal spring and a geyser in active eruption is very marked, but between the two there is every grade of action. Some geysers appear as quiet springs, as for instance the Grand Geyser during its period of quiescence. Others might easily be mistaken for constantly boiling springs, as in the case of the Giant Geyser, in which the water is constantly in active ebullition. This is true also of the Strockr of Iceland. Many of the springs, therefore, that in the Yellowstone Park have been classed as constantly boiling springs may be unsuspected geysers. The Excelsior Geyser was not discovered to be a geyser until eight years after the setting aside of the park. Almost all constantly boiling springs have periods of increased activity, and those which spurt a few feet into the air have been classed as pseudo-geysers.

"It has been noticed that geysers occur where the intensity of volcanic action is decreasing. In the neighborhood of active volcanoes, such as

Vesuvius, the temperature appears to be too high, and the vapor escapes as steam from what are called stufas. When the rocks at the surface are more cooled the water comes forth in liquid form.

"We will now pass to the various geyser theories that have been proposed by different writers."

Dr. Peal then proceeds to give the theories of Sir J. Herschell and Sir George McKenzie, but as they are accepted and extended by others, we may pass on to Bischof's, of which Dr. Peal says: "Very similar to McKenzie's theory is the one adopted by Bischof in his Researches on the Internal Heat of the Globe (pages 227, 228). It is really the theory of Krug Von Nidda, who examined the geyser in 1833. Bischof says:

"'He (Krug Von Nidda) takes it for granted that these hot springs derive their temperature from the aqueous vapors rising from below. When these vapors are able to rise freely in a continued column the water at the different depths must have a constant temperature equal to that at which water would boil under the pressure existing at the respective depths; hence the constant ebullition of the permanent springs and their boiling heat. If, on the other hand, the vapors be prevented by the complicated windings of its channels from rising to the surface; if, for example, they be arrested in caverns, the temperature in the upper layers of water must necessarily become reduced, because a large quantity of it is lost by evaporation at the surface, which cannot be replaced from below. And any circulation of the layers of water at different temperatures, by reason of their unequal specific gravities, seems to be very much interrupted by the narrowness and sinuousity of the passage. The intermitting springs of Iceland are probably caused by the existence of caverns, in which the vapor is retained by the pressure of the column of water in the channel which leads to the surface. Here this vapor collects, and presses the water in the cavern downward until its elastic force becomes sufficiently great to effect a passage through the column of water which confines it. The violent escape of the vapor causes the thunder-like subterranean sound and the trembling of the earth which precedes each eruption. The vapors do not appear at the surface until they have heated the water to their own temperature.

" 'When so much vapor has escaped that the expansive force of that which remains has become less than the pressure of the confining column of water, tranquility is restored, and this lasts until such a quantity of vapor is again collected as to produce a fresh eruption. The spouting of the spring is therefore repeated at intervals, depending on the capacity of the cavern, the height of the column of water, and the heat generated below.'" Dr. Peal continues:

" Bishof says that the eruptions of the Geyser and Strockr agree exactly with this explanation and he accounts for the two distinct classes of eruption observed in the Geyser as follows:

"'The two distinct classes of eruption in the geyser which we have already mentioned seem to be attributable to two different cavities. A small cavity fills quicker, and, therefore, empties itself more frequently; a larger one fills slower, empties itself seldomer, but with greater violence.' "

Bunsen's theory is the next considered and is somewht similar to Bischof's but with notable differences.   After taking temperatures at different points in the Geyser tube his first conclusions are that:

(1) The temperature in the geyser tube increases as we descend.

(2) At no point does the water in the tube attain the temperature of ebullition which it should have under the pressure to which it is subjected, but the temperature depends on the time that has elapsed since the last eruption. As a great eruption comes near it approaches the boiling point.

(3) At the depth of about forty-five feet the difference between the temperature of the water

and the calculated boiling point for that pressure is the least.

The main point of his theory appears to be that an eruption takes place when the water in the tube reaches the boiling point, and to account for it, "He supposes that the column in the central tube communicates by a long and sinuous channel with some space, be it what it may, which is subjected to the action of the direct source of subterranean heat. The temperature gets raised above the boiling point, due to the pressure, and a sudden generation of steam is the result. This steam rises in the column of water, which, being cooler, causes it to condense. Gradually the heat of the water is raised until the water of the channel must boil, and the steam therefore cannot condense, but must accumulate and acquire a gradually increasing tension. The condensation of the bubbles possesses a periodic character, and to this is due the uplifting of the water in what Bunsen calls conical water hills, which are accompanied by the subterranean explosions."

Prof. Comstock is quoted as thinking "Bunsen's theory has not yet been proved adequate to explain the more prominent features of geyser eruptions. Nor does it, in his opinion, account for all the differences between geysers and hot springs, and he proposes a structural hypothesis which combines Bischof's and Bunsen's theories.''

This hypothesis is illustrated by a figure in which a reservoir partly filled with water is connected with the surface by a tube having a double curve, and he explains that the water collecting in the depressed curve should confine the steam, rising from the reservoir in the other curve until the pressure is sufficient to cause an eruption. His theory of action being that the water in the reservoir remains in equilibrium at a certain level, and the constant heat fills the space above with vapor, which heats the water held in the downward bend of the tube, and that also evolves vapor which fills the balance of the tube to the vent. When the combined pressure of this vapor and water are overcome by the expansion of vapor accumulated above the reservoir, they are forced out, and followed by a portion of the water of the reservoir. This theory is in the report of Captain Jones on Northwestern Wyoming.

The last theory cited by Dr. Peal is that of S. Baring-Gould, "Who visited the Iceland geysers in 1863, and thinks that a bent tube is sufficient to explain the action of the Great Geyser. He took an iron tube and bent it in an angle of 110°, keeping one arm half the length of the other. He filled the tube with water and placed the short arm in the fire. For a moment the surface of the liquid remained quiet, and then the pipe began to quiver; a slight overflow took place, without any sign of ebullition, and then suddenly, with a throb, the whole column was forced high into the air. With a tube, the long arm of which measured two feet and the bore of which was three-eighths of an inch, he sent a jet to the height of eighteen feet. Steam is generated in the short arm and presses down the water, causing an overflow until the steam bubble turns the angle, when it forces out the column in the long arm with incredible violence."

Dr. Peal now goes on to say:

" Of the theories that we have just enumerated, perhaps no one is adequate to explain all the phenomena of geyser action. Bunsen's theory comes nearest to it, and in the simplest kinds of geysers is a sufficient explanation. The variations and modifications in the geyser tubes and subterranean water passages must undoubtedly be important factors entering into any complete explanation of geyser action. Now, of course, we can see what the conditions are at the surface, but in our experiments we can penetrate to a very inconsiderable distance. We have, therefore, no data to present on these points, and investigations of this branch of the subject will have to be carried on in an artificial manner; that is artificial geysers

will have to be constructed, and various modifications made in the tubes until results are
reached analogous to those seen in natural geysers. If water in a glass tube be heated with
rapidity from the bottom, it will be expelled
from the tube violently, and if boiled in a ket-
tle which has a lid and a spout, either the lid
will be blown off or the water will be forced out
through the spout. The first case is an illustration, in part at least, of Bunsen's theory,
and the second exemplifies the theories which
presuppose the existence of subterranean cavities with tubes at or near the surface. According to the former we must suppose that the
layer of rock, extending seventy-five to
seventy-seven feet below the surface, contains
sufficient heat to account for geyseric phenomena; or else that the geyser tube has some opening, either at the bottom or on the sides, by
which steam and superheated water have access
to it from a considerably greater depth where
the temperature is very high. At these depths
caverns probably exist."   *   *   *   *

"That such cavities exist is more than probable. On page 405 I have indicated my belief,
that all geysers are originally due to a violent
outburst of steam and water, and under such
conditions, irregular cavities and passages are
more likely to be formed than regular tubes." * *

" In view of what we have just written, Bunsen's conclusion (No. 2) would have to be modified somewhat. His conclusion was that at no point in the tube did the water attain the temperature of ebullition which it should have under the pressure to which it is subjected. As far as this relates to the straight tube in which his temperatures were taken, it may be so; but if he could have taken temperatures in the side conduit, I have little doubt he would soon have reached a point where the temperature would not only be at the boiling point for that depth but even exceed it. In the Yellowstone Park we obtained a number of surface temperatures which were above the boiling point. In the Great Geyser of Iceland, the mass of water in the tube prevents this condition at the surface, and when it takes place opposite the aperture an eruption is caused. In the main, however, I am inclined to accept Bunsen's theory, especially as it seems to me to require subterranean cavities in which the water must be heated. Whether these are caverns, enlargements of tubes, or sinus channels, appears to me to be of no consequence, except as the interval or period of the geyser might be affected by the form of the reservoir holding the water."

Dr. Peal has reached conclusions which present an imaginary picture of the interior structure of the great geysers of the Park, that bears a striking resemblance to what the two caves of

the Black Hills prove to be the true conditions;
although it is evident he had in mind caverns
of no such vast extent, nor of so complicated a
system of cavities and tubes. He overlooked an
important feature, however, in not accepting
Professor Comstock's idea of the tube having a
double curve. The double curve is, or was,
conspicuous in both the caves. Unfortunately,
its perfection in Wind Cave was necessarily partially sacrificed to make the passage traversable
for visitors; but in describing the enormous
labor of opening up the cave, Mr. McDonald
showed how an arching "crawl" had been
worked down by blasting, and the depression beyond filled to raise it to the desired level for
securing the present easy passage at the bottom of the main tube, which is the entrance
passage. This double curve in the tube is simply the rough original of the S trap of sanitary
plumbing. In both caves it is somewhat irregular and deformed, but the familiar "trap" is
easily recognized. The destruction of one of
the Yellowstone geysers was, no doubt,
due to the breaking of the S. One of the many
reasons for establishing military control over
the Park is said to have been the disastrous
results following the introduction of a large
quantity of soap into the geyser to cause a pre-
mature eruption. The impatience of the party
was rewarded by an eruption accompanied by

explosions that shook the earth for a great distance, and the geyser has not been seen in action since.

Dr. Peal finds the theories advanced for the generation of steam unsatisfactory and insufficient, especially in the class of geysers having a long steam period. He says: (page 423)

"The Castle Geyser differs from Old Faithful and the Bee Hive mainly in the fact that it has a long steam period, during which the steam pours out or is pushed from the geyser throat with great violence and a terrific noise. There appear to be only two possible explanations of this difference, viz., either an accumulation of immense volumes of steam in the Castle, or an instantaneous formation of steam throughout the length of the geyser tube. The former, to our mind, is untenable, because it seems impossible that the water, which is exhausted in fifteen minutes, should exert enough power to keep down the immense amount of steam that escapes for more than an hour. According to Bunsen's theory, it can be readily explained. The relief afforded by the first part of the eruptions allows the superheated water to rise rapidly, and before it can reach the top or orifice of the tube it is all converted into steam from the top downward with inconceivable rapidity, and must be forced out with the terrific violence which is noted in the case of the Castle.

On page 208 we have expressed the opinion that
it is the oldest geyser in the region, and it seems
to us that a greater length in the tube, with a
consequent greater supply of water, will account
for the difference between the Castle and Old
Faithful, the latter of which we consider one of
the youngest geysers in the Upper Geyser Basin.''

A study of the Caves in connection with the
active Geysers indicates that the theory he suggests and then rejects, is probably the true
explanation of the difference between the two
kinds of geysers. It seems that the length of
the tube must necessarily have more effect on
the height of the jet than on the generation of
steam; as after an eruption the tube is hotter
than at any other time and therefore the generation of steam in it should be less than usual,
unless the fresh inflow of water was cold. Then
if the storage cavities are broad but low, the
steam cannot accumulate above the water; but
when the pressure becomes sufficient to force a
passage through the tube, the water and steam
are expelled together until the pressure is
exhausted. But if the storage chambers are
vertical fissures, as Wind Cave illustrates, vast
quantities of steam must accumulate above the
water level in the main reservoirs before the
pressure can become sufficient to expel the
water in the tube, after which steam alone
continues to rush out until the pressure is so

relieved that it can no longer force a passage through the water remaining in the trap, when quiet is restored. By the constant addition of fresh water from the surface, by percolation or other usual ways of sinking, the necessary conditions for the generation of steam are maintained with surprising regularity.

The differences in the shape and general arrangement of the cavities and tubes of the two caves, indicate that their action as geysers was very unlike. Wind Cave evidently sent a rather slender column to a great height, nearly perpendicular, and the water eruption was followed by a long steam period. Crystal Cave ejected a much larger jet more frequently, at a low angle of inclination, the eruption was sooner over, and was not followed by a steam period of any consequence.

Thus it can be seen that the caves of the Black Hills prove the theories in regard to geyser action in Yellowstone Park, and those theories, in turn, prove the past history of the caves. The study of geyser action also shows that the conical or dome shape of some of the cave chambers is not due to the whirl of incoming floods, as in other regions, but to jets of water forced up from lower levels.

Perhaps the finest geyser basin, and possible cave, ever in existence was destroyed when the Grand Cañon of the Yellowstone became a cañon.

Evidences of the former conditions in control of this gorgeously brilliant scene are neither wanting nor doubtful. Steam constantly issues from numerous small vents in the cañon walls, and a field glass reveals miniature geysers in action down in the depth of the cañon, nearly half a mile below the top of the wall; while the entire cañon shows, in both the color and character of its rocks, that chemical agencies have wrought changes here that have not been effected in other exposures of similar nature. It seems not improbable that the relation of Yellowstone River to the Grand Cañon was the same as, at the present time, is that of the Firehole to the Upper, Middle, and Lower Geyser Basins: and that an explosion of great force was followed by a gen eral collapse instead of the usual eruption of one of the grandest geysers; one result being the sudden precipitation of the river into a new, beautiful, and totally unexpected channel. After its great leap of two hundred and ninety-seven* feet at the Lower Fall, the river flows in a brilliant, narrow line of emerald green, broken by the white foam of frequent cascades, between magnificent walls of yellow, white, pink, and red of most vivid hues.

*Measurement by the Hayden Party.

THE END.

www.ingramcontent.com/pod-product-compliance
Lightning Source LLC
Chambersburg PA
CBHW031332070726
47496CB00018B/1828